Bede's Way

a novel by
Joe Stewart
www.bede-trilogy.weebly.com

edited by
Pam Stewart

Cover Photo of
St. Bede the venerable scholar
reproduced by kind permission of
Mgr. John Ryan at St Bede's Rotherham.
Design by Pendle Stained Glass Ltd

St Bede the venerable scholar
Pendle Stained Glass Ltd

Forward

This third book in the series traces the journey of the Codex Amiatinus to Rome and Bede's possible role in that journey. These books are not meant to be historically factually correct. They are a fiction or perhaps a faction; loosely based on factual events. They contain anachronisms; both intentional and accidental. In fact the term Codex Amiatinus, mentioned in my previous book Bede's World, is such an anachronism; did you spot it? Bede would not have used such a term, as the title is derived from Monte Amiata in Italy where the Codex was discovered in the 9th century. He may have used the term Codex for his work, it is derived from the Latin caudex (meaning tree trunk) which would have been used for wooden tablets. He certainly uses Codex in this book as a means of ease of reference.

It has always been my intention to write uplifting stories incorporating biblical references. This story may be a little darker than the first two but I trust it remains faithful to the spirit of Bede.

I hope you enjoy my tales of Bede of Jarrow and Monkwearmouth, a true giant in the annals of Christianity in Northumbria and the world.

Joe Stewart
www.bede-trilogy.weebly.com
Twitter - @bedethree
Email – bedetrilogy@outlook.com

Contents

Chapter One
The Cleadon Hills

I am walking the well trodden path between Jarrow and Monkwearmouth. A path worn brown and hard by the feet of thousands of passing souls. A way for holy pilgrims between those two harbours of Christianity. It is their way and it is my way; it is Bede's Way.

Since you last heard of me walking this way, much water has flowed down the Wear, as well as the Don, the Tyne tributary which flows past my cell window at Jarrow and into the main river. Many summers have passed too. In fact, as many as twenty of God's four seasons, full of promise, have flowed through my life. Blessed years, as fulsome as the great waterways of the Kingdom of Northumbria, gushing their life-giving unction. The years, though, have not been without their times of drought and sadnesses.

I sit by the derelict windmill on top of the hill, long since vacated by my father's erstwhile friend, Jonathan. The torn sails wail their lament for the late miller, as the north easterly breeze whistles through the blackened blistered cloth. The innovative superstructure, which once could rotate through three hundred and sixty degrees in order to take advantage of the prevailing winds, now sits uneasily at an angle to the base of the windmill, having been derailed from the track which guided the castors on its circular journey. My father's design has been imitated and replicated many times throughout the north and indeed the country. How he would have been disappointed to see his prototype so ill used and unappreciated. The rails, rusted and broken, never to be used for their original purpose, serve only to make the tilting building even more dangerous.

Nevertheless the view from its vantage point, at the pinnacle of the Cleadon Hills, could never be destroyed by time's unerring onslaught and, as I stand and drink in the vista, I breathe deeply of the spring air and call to my young companion, frolicking on the grassy bank below me.

"Mika! Come on lad, time to eat. We've been travelling well over two hours and I think we still have a further hour to go." In fact, as I have travelled this lane many times, I know precisely how long we have left to travel and it is nearer to two hours than the hour I told my fellow traveller. In deference to his youth I deliberately chose to underestimate the time remaining, in order to act as a sort of encouragement for him. I hope the Good Lord does not judge me too severely for this deception but it is for the most honourable of motives that I do this, in order to act as an incentive for the boy to complete his first journey to Monkwearmouth. The boy in question was none other than my good friend Odin's eleven year old son. Born ten months after I had officiated at his father and mother's wedding in St Paul's Monastery Jarrow, the young lad had just recently become linked to our community on the same part time basis I had originally joined. Like me, Mika had showed more promise than some of his contemporaries and so I had suggested to Odin that he should be educated by the monks. Odin and his wife Rowena were reluctant to lose the service of their son and, although both Christian, were not sure they wished him to commit his future to the monastery. After reassuring them that there was no ulterior motive to my offer and that the tuition would be on a part time basis, so he could continue with his family chores, they agreed to my proposal.

"Brother Bede, what is this place? It looks old and dilapidated." panted the boy and before waiting for an explanation continued. "I've been practising some of my training routines for our kickbladder team. We've got a big game coming up soon." His enthusiasm was infectious and I well remembered the times his father, Joseph and I lived for the game.

"Aye son! Your dad and your Uncle Joseph could teach you a few things about kickbladder. And I wasn't a bad player too!" I could see from the incredulous look on his face, that the prospect of so decrepit a group of adults being able to play 'the beautiful game', as he called it, was remote indeed. "Here get that down you. You must be famished after that walk." I unfurled a white cloth to reveal some bread and cheese and broke the loaf, ensuring that Mika received the lion's share. I repeated the process with the cheese and before too long the lad was chomping away on the makeshift lunch. I passed him a gourd of water and he glugged down the refreshing liquid, product of my own holy well.

"The owner of this old mill was Jonathan, one of my father's many friends. In fact my dad built this windmill and that superstructure there could be turned in any direction to catch the prevailing wind. Now, since Jonathan's death, it is a shadow of its former self. It is so sad to see. Of course there are other mills along the coast which are still producing flour but this old building stands alone and unloved." I could see my words were lost on Mika and he seemed impatient to resume our journey. "Come on then Mika. Let's get going. Here! Don't forget your satchels." I passed the boy two brown leather pouches and made sure that they were held securely across his chest. The contents were most precious and were the object of our visit to our sister, or should I say mother, house in Monkwearmouth. Satisfied that he was aware of the importance of our mission and that he bore the weight of responsibility well, I invited him to proceed. I carried a third satchel which had held our lunch and some additional, minor documents bound for the same destination. Buoyed by the rest and food, we made our way down the grassy hillside toward the coast that would eventually lead to our ultimate destination. Half way down the hill the path kinked its way to the right and we both stopped to survey the scene before us. Stretching out from where we stood, the fields carpeted their way down to the sea, shimmering in the distance like an azure linen sheet. Mika gazing towards the horizon exclaimed:

"He gathered the oceans into a single place; he put the deep water into storehouses. Let all the world fear the Lord; let all the inhabitants of the world stand in awe of him."

I smiled back at him in recognition of a job well accomplished, "Ah! Well done Mika I am glad you have remembered your lessons on the Psalms and I concur with your sentiments. I have walked this way many times and I never tire of the sight which meets our eyes at this point. Indeed it is a confirmation of the glory of our God and I am pleased that, on your first journey to Monkwearmouth, it has made such a profound effect upon you."

We continued the journey to the coast, singing some of the Psalms in our Gregorian plain chant, which we use in our worship in the monastery. I am afraid I may have been too pedantic about the finer points of the descants and harmonies and felt he was losing interest in our pastime. I decided to change the subject and engage him in telling me about his interests. This consisted mainly of his kickbladder exploits and how he hoped his team would win the annual tournament which takes place at the old Roman ruins at Arbeia in South Shields around Pentecost time. To his utter surprise I regaled him with stories of how I, his father and his Uncle Joseph had taken part and indeed had won the inaugural competition some twenty or so summers ago. He was fascinated to hear how girls had featured prominently in our team and he confessed his reticence at having to include them in his line-up. Although the rules regarding the inclusion of females had not changed, it seemed (unfortunately) that male attitudes towards their counterparts and potential teammates hadn't either!

As we made our way to the Bents Cottages at the sea front, I said a little prayer in remembrance of my father's two late friends who used to inhabit the small fishing cottage. I recalled the meal of fish I had enjoyed with the pair, the final time I was to meet them before hearing of their demise. On subsequent visits to Monkwearmouth the cottage had grown increasingly dilapidated and the hull of the late fisherman's small boat lay rotting in the sand, the brown woods like the ribs of a beached whale. But as we approached I could see signs of activity in the building and, as a young man stopped his work to acknowledge our presence, I returned his greeting,

"Good morning young man, I am Bede. I knew well the previous occupants of this home, Ozzie and Ena, good friends of my late father. I was sad to see the old place going to ruin but I am pleased that it looks to be occupied once again." The young man confirmed that he and his wife and two children would be moving in soon and apologised for his lack of hospitality because of the current poor state of the building but offered us some liquid refreshment, which we were glad of. So we sat around a makeshift table and our new acquaintance poured some mead from a gourd which had previously hung from a nearby doorpost. I motioned towards my young companion and he realised instinctively that I was referring to the alcoholic strength of the beverage and he duly added a little water to the lad's drink.

He made his introductions and said he knew of me by reputation and asked if I would return when he had completed his work, in order to invoke God's blessing upon his homestead. I agreed wholeheartedly and was also pleased to learn that he too would be supporting his family from the sea and so the legacy of Ozzie and Ena is preserved and continued. We bade our farewells in order to complete the last leg of our journey in time for the evening meal at Monkwearmouth. This intelligence was sufficient to encourage a fresh spring in the step of my companion and we duly came upon our destination.

So, my dear reader, you may think that things are as ever they were and similar in many ways to the story I told you previously. The repetitive cycle of the days turning unerringly on to eternity. But my dear friend, things are not so idyllic. My story is one of intrigue and deception and of possible betrayal and yes, I believe, even murder!

Chapter Two
Monkwearmouth

Monkwearmouth glowed in the early evening sunlight, the great orange orb, two thirds protruding above the westerly horizon, providing a halo of holy light around the outline of the monastery. It would shortly seek its night time shelter beneath the rolling green hills, allowing the starry ink like sea of sky to invade its daytime domain. The hills and buildings of the Sunter Land and St. Peter's would then be clothed in darkness, wrapped in a black shroud, whilst the sun sought out new lands to bathe in its warming rays.

My companion and I made our way from the mouth of the river and passed by the glassworks, still belching fire from its furnace, used to transform sand into that thin transparent protector from the elements. Such a delicate, fragile substance, yet strong enough to withstand all that the north wind can throw at it. And still it is able to allow the image of the Creator's work to permeate it, be it land or seascape. The glass workers could be seen at their toil, stripped naked to the waist, their day's hard work evidenced by the glint of sweat on their lithe torsos. The track we took had been made more permanent and resistant to the weather by the application of spent ash from the work's furnace. How pleasing to see such a waste product put to such a useful purpose. Our feet crushed the ash even more firmly in its place as we made our contribution, through use, to the construction of the walk way. Hopefully numerous descendants would benefit from our toil and the way of I, Bede, would become even more famed. The cessation of the sound of crunching under foot heralded the end of our journey and the arrival at our holy destination.

We were welcomed warmly by Brother Stephen, the guest master who is responsible for monitoring the comings and goings in the monastery. He informed us that our arrival was expected and took from us our satchels containing our precious cargo. He told us that these would be taken to Abbot Ceolfrith's study where he would meet with us next morning after the Eucharist. Our esteemed leader was engaged in important community business and this would be the earliest opportunity we would have to speak with him. Stephen said he had been told by the abbot that their meeting was to be without interruption and so had set aside the whole morning for this purpose. He then suggested that I adjourn to my own cell whilst Mika would be led to one of the guest cells. Looking a little anxious at this suggestion, the boy was quickly reassured when I said we would soon meet again for our evening meal following Vespers. Anticipating that his hunger would be satiated by the reputed generous helpings which St. Peter's Monkwearmouth was noted for, he followed the young monk deputed to help him and was gone from my sight.

I have a personal room, or cell as we call them, at both Monkwearmouth and Jarrow, as I divide my time between both houses. I would estimate that I spend more time at Jarrow at the moment, as the slower pace of life is more conducive to my scholarly work. The work, which is the subject of this current meeting with Ceolfrith, has been all consuming of late and has required a milieu of tranquillity. This may seem a little incongruous to you, dear reader, that there can be such a difference in atmosphere between the two houses dedicated to the worship of God. But Monkwearmouth is not just a place of worship and learning, it is almost a city in its own right. With its own bakery, butchery and land set aside for crops, it is indeed a mighty commercial force in the area, employing many people from the local community.

Since the attack of plague struck (which hit Jarrow more than it did Monkwearmouth) God has blessed our community with more vocations. Our numbers have grown to nearly seven hundred at Monkwearmouth and nearly one hundred at Jarrow. Some of our brothers will be moving shortly to help Wilfred establish a community at Hexham. This has caused a little consternation amongst our community, with some of the more ambitious brothers seeing it as an opportunity to further their careers. Wilfred has progressed in the Church (as many thought he would) becoming Bishop of York, not though without making many enemies along the way. You may remember how forthright he was in his views when he was with us at Monkwearmouth. This continued at Whitby, with Hilda struggling to contain him, and at York where he became bishop. He is an ambitious man, not only for himself, but also for the things of God but his native

Northumbria was never far from his heart and he wished to establish an abbey at Hexham, which he was given leave to do so. Wilfred is from a well to do Northumbrian family and began his studies at Lindisfarne. Although a Celt, like me, in spirit he has always been a vocal advocate for the Roman position in the Church today. This dichotomy between the Celtic and Roman practice within the Church has threatened to divide it. However Wilfred believes that we should use the remnants of the Roman Empire as a means of furthering the Gospel's progress throughout the world. There are also signs of him using his noble ancestry to promote his beliefs and both these opinions have been responsible for his mixed popularity amongst his confrères.

The community here at Monkwearmouth has become extremely wealthy, with over one thousand head of cattle. This provides more than our need of milk and meat, as well as providing us with velum. We also own what seems an incalculable amount of sheep, supplying us with wool and meat. Not the most intelligent of animals, local shepherds are employed to care for them. We are able to sell our produce locally as well as providing for those peasants who are not able to feed their families. Monkwearmouth, and Jarrow to a lesser extent, are integral and invaluable commercial enterprises and the local economy hinges on the welfare of these houses.

There is very little difference in my Monkwearmouth and Jarrow cells, save for the view from my windows. Although Church glass is stained with vivid colours and depicts scenes from the Holy Scriptures, my cell window is clear glass, providing a more copious view of the Wear's watery mouth to the east and the Sunter Land to the west. Directly across from my cell I can see the workers in Jean's boatyard. It is a view usually full of activity on and off the river. Whereas the view from my Jarrow cell is a little more bucolic, with sheep gently nibbling the grass and the Don tributary meandering its way to the Tyne. Both cells are sparsely furnished, with a wooden bed, a table (which doubles as a desk) and a chair, all overseen by a simple wooden cross on the wall.

Two bowls of piping hot water are brought to my cell. I plunge my feet immediately into one, to relieve the exertions of the day, whilst the other cools on the table. After drying my feet with the cloth provided, I use the other bowl for the rest of my ablutions. Having been cleansed from the dust and sweat of my endeavours I feel like a new man and ready to face my brother monks. A cleric's life like mine is ruled by bells (as well as the Rule of St Benedict and of course mainly the Lord Jesus Christ himself) and these give a routine and structure to the day. The bell I am hearing now invites me to the service of sung Vespers in our chapel and then afterwards to our evening meal in the cavernous refectory reached from the church via the sacristy. I process into the chapel with my brother monks, each joining the phalanx of men returning to the body of the church from whatever activity they were engaged in, be it spiritual or temporal, until we are nearly five hundred strong in the knave of the church. The absentees accounted for by those on duties deemed too important to leave and secondments to other houses or working in the community. Father Abbot's absence was due to the former reason.

Ceolfrith's non-appearance at the service continued during the preparation for our meal, as we all sat in our pre-ordained places on the somewhat uncomfortable refectory benches. This discomfort was not due to the hardness or quality of the wood from which they were made, nor the workmanship of the carpenters. Quite the contrary! The skill of the woodworker was evident from the precision with which they had accomplished their end product. Joints dovetailed perfectly and the lacquered smooth finish would caress the roundest of bottoms. No it was the fact that the seats were without a back to them that made them so uncomfortable. Monks would perch on the benches, turning this disadvantage into a positive by using it as the opportunity to improve their posture and sit bolt upright like proud soldiers. Others would admit defeat and slouch over their meals, not able to exert the same self control over their bodies as their more erect colleagues.

I could see that Mika was a little embarrassed at the sight of so many of us routinely going about the business of the preparation for dining whilst he could only stand, paralysed, awaiting direction. This eventually came in the form of another young monk, himself a fairly new recruit to monastic life, who, realising Mika's predicament, escorted the boy to a table reserved for guests. Although this time of readiness was meant to be in silence, as was our meal, in reality it was done to the accompaniment of shuffling feet, the screech of benches being pulled out and drawn in again, and coughing. Eventually this background noise subsided and, as Ceolfrith was not present, Father Prior said grace with the final amen being the signal for those serving to begin their duties. It only remained to see who would be reading the scriptural passage during our repast.

Ah! Brother Anselm is going to read for us at our meal. A loyal servant of Christ and the Benedictine Order; a service of sixty years, more if you include his boyhood period of instruction. A man well into his eighties, his tall thin frame now bowed with age. A slight build that belies a stentorian voice which can still traverse the length and breadth of the refectory, awakening even the most somnolent of listeners from their prandial concerns. He stumbles his way up the oak staircase, it's gnarled wood complementing his work worn hands. His skin blotched brown and creased like an untidy stained tablecloth. Having reached the summit he leans on the pulpit wall, thankful of its support and wheezes. Taking what seems an interminable time to recover his breath (almost to the point of concern) he drew himself up to his full height and announced he would be reading from the Book of Psalms; Psalm 19 to be precise. This news is very pleasing to my ears. The Book of Psalms is my favourite book of Holy Scripture, save for the Gospels, and I eagerly await his retelling. He begins:

"Give thanks to the Lord, for he is good; his love endures forever.
Let Israel say: "His love endures forever."
Let the house of Aaron say: "His love endures forever."
Let those who fear the Lord say: "His love endures forever."

When hard pressed, I cried to the Lord; he brought me into a spacious place. The Lord is with me, I will not be afraid. What can mere mortals do to me? The Lord is with me, he is my helper. I look in triumph on my enemies.

It is better to take refuge in the Lord than to trust in princes.
All the nations surrounded me but in the name of the Lord I cut them down. They surrounded me on every side but in the name of the Lord I cut them down. They swarmed around me like bees but they were consumed

as quickly as burning thorns, in the name of the Lord I cut them down."

Anselm's voice was strong and urgent, building steadily to a crescendo as he related the trials the psalmist had undergone. Having stirred in us a sense of empathy for the hard done to writer of the psalm, his voice softens and mellows, yet still has the power to carry to each and every one of his listeners, as he continues:

"I was pushed back and about to fall but the Lord helped me.
The Lord is my strength and my defence, he has become my salvation.
Shouts of joy and victory resound in the tents of the righteous:
The Lord's right hand is lifted high, the Lord's right hand has done mighty things!"

With that he gently closed the book, turned and tentatively made his way back down the steps and returned to his solitary place to the rear of the refectory, where he had projected those words of God's greatness. He preferred this lonely situation where he could eat his meal in peace and reflect upon the words he had just read. Anselm was the second most senior monk in our community. Actually he was the most senior here at Monkwearmouth but found himself junior, by about six months, to one of my erstwhile mentors, Xaviour, at Jarrow. Their good natured rivalry regarding their seniority, could be misunderstood as dislike, by the uninformed observer. But anyone spending any amount of time in their presence knew this to be a thinly disguised front for a mutual respect and admiration for one another. We completed our meal in silence and I could see that Mika received extra helpings from the monks on serving duty and I smiled as a second or third portion of apple pie was devoured by the lad. I raised my eyebrows in exclamation and from his expression I could see that he had received my implied rebuke, as he declined further offers of food.

After the meal there followed a time of social communal activities in our common room where tit bits of gossip were exchanged and updates given on projects undertaken. As ever I find that I am the subject of much interest, having to impart news from Jarrow. Most of it quite prosaic, as I relate how this one has done such and such a thing and that one did that sort of thing. Some of which I feel I have already imparted and it takes a measure of patience to recall these self same events. It is, though, good to have this time to talk and everyone looks forward to it. However I found a subtle difference in the attitude of some of the brothers who were due to be seconded to Wilfred's abbey in Hexham.

Perhaps I am being over-sensitive but I thought I detected a cooling towards me. Many of the monks had worked up in Hexham helping to build the crypt. Apparently they had 'acquired' stones from the old Roman settlement at Corstopitum in order to build the chapel in the crypt. The main body of the abbey is being built above it. I happened to say that, whatever the faults of the Romans, the remains of their buildings were worthy of preservation, both from architectural and cultural viewpoints. I was taken aback at the strength of derision my view was met with. Some of the monks were quite vociferous in their objections to my opinion with one monk in particular, Sixtus, being particularly vehement. Wilfred's discipline is notoriously lax and I have heard he allows his monks to drink more mead and wine than Ceolfrith does. Rumour has it that some monks have been known to be drunk which has led to much bad example given to other younger monks and the laity.

Sixtus is a tall brute of a man (though God knows I should not be his judge) who you would not wish to cross swords with, both literally and metaphorically. He pressed home his argument that we should have no respect for our former unwelcome occupiers and that a number of his family had suffered at the hands of the Romans in the past. This was to disregard the fact that this alleged transgression must have taken place well over a century ago and took little account of our Lord's injunction to not just forgive our enemies but love them and pray for those who hurt us. I thought better of trying to remind my brother monk of this command to love and at the end of the evening we agreed to differ and concluded the day by praising God in our final service of Compline. Having humbled ourselves before our Creator we retired to our cells and, after a period of personal prayer, I slept.

Chapter Three
Ceolfrith

Ceolfrith was elected abbot after the death of Abbot Benet. The abbot has overall responsibility for the monastery including the material and spiritual well-being of the monks and those who work alongside them. He is also responsible for all financial aspects of the monastery. He has a council of monks to advise and support him as he seeks to be a true father to the monastery. The abbot is elected by those monks who are solemnly professed and he serves for eight years before seeking re-election or retirement. Ceolfrith was a worthy successor to Benet and was a well respected monk.

I met Ceolfrith next morning, as arranged, in his study situated in that part of the monastery with an upper level. On this floor is a library and two study rooms, the larger being the working domain of Father Abbot and he was invariably to be found here, about the monastery's business, most of the day. The second was the lair of Father Prior, second in command to Ceolfrith, but he was rarely to be found at his desk. Father Prior's role was to be the 'finger on the pulse' of the community and so he has become the eminence grise of the monastery, appearing at the most unexpected of moments to ensure all the brothers were gainfully employed and engaged in the ultimate task of proclaiming God's Kingdom here on earth.

Often in a religious community there is a tension between the two top men, with each striving to establish their own brand of Christianity amongst the brotherhood. But no such tension exists between Ceolfrith and his deputy Father Prior, Hwaetberht. Ceolfrith was so adept at man management and always believed in promoting the right man for the job, irrespective of his personal feelings towards the candidate. This has led to many a sworn enemy being won over to his cause and becoming his most loyal ally, if not his friend.

I ascended to his study up a grand stone staircase. From the landing a corridor, to the left, led to the two studies with the library off to the right. It was well stocked with literature and books brought by Benet and Ceolfrith from their many travels throughout Europe. Even I had added to their number with some of my scholarly work. However as Jesus said, *"a profit is without acclaim in his own land"* and so I have had very little recognition for my work within my own community. I feel only my old friends Godric and Ceolfrith really appreciate what I am doing. Ceolfrith always reassures me and tells me not to worry, as recognition within the wider world will come one day. Off the library is the Scriptorium, which now is seldom used here at Monkwearmouth, as the main work of scribing is done in my Jarrow Scriptorium. However it is here that I find Father Abbot.

Ceolfrith is poring over a myriad of velum parchments, spread out, seemingly haphazardly, across many tables. Some obviously commandeered for the purpose from other parts of the monastery. He had almost a manic look, as his eyes darted from one parchment to another. His bearing was nervous and his appearance rather unkempt, with bags under his eyes betraying his lack of sleep. He was preoccupied with the task in front of him and did not mark my entrance with his usual warm greeting. Instead he stroked his thin beard with his hand, conspiratorially, as if planning a course of action. Finally he showed some recognition of my presence and nodded in my direction, as if to say he did not wish his train of thought to be interrupted. The parchments he was so diligently scrutinising, were none other than the precious cargo Mika and I had born across the hills in our leather satchels.

Whenever we were in a formal setting within the monastery I always addressed Ceolfrith by his title of Father Abbot but in informal or private situations I used his Christian name, as befits our long standing friendship, and it was by this epithet I address him now.

"My dear Ceolfrith, you seem fatigued, have you not slept well?"

"Brother Bede I have not slept at all since you brought these holy works of art to me, the final pieces of our Codex. They are magnificent Bede, you and the brothers in the Scriptorium have indeed worked hard and under the influence of the Holy Spirit. They are clearly a work of that Spirit of God which was bestowed upon the apostles at that first Pentecost. Previously timid and fearful of the merest shadow, they became so emboldened that they spoke out without fear or trepidation. They spoke languages they had not previously had knowledge of to the many cosmopolitan people assembled for the harvest. As many as three thousand believers were added to their number." Ceolfrith was in full flow, as if inspired himself by his own personal Pentecost and, stopping only momentarily to draw breath, he continued, "You, Bede my son, will so inspire many more believers by your work as blessed by the Spirit of Jesus, our one true Saviour. This translation will form the basis for many future translations of the Gospel, and it will be modified and re-translated for unknown future generations. I applaud you Bede and your confrères in the Scriptorium and I ask most earnestly that you pass on my thanks to them."

The works he was referring to are the last books in the Latin Vulgate version of my Bible translation from Jerome's version, which he translated from the Hebrew. This Codex was commissioned by the late Pope Gregory, who did not live long enough to appreciate our labours. But I know Ceolfrith hopes that the current Pope and namesake Gregory the Second, will be the recipient of the completed work. I felt my cheeks reddening and also a pang of guilt entered my soul as the sin of pride began to surface. I chose my reply as best I could,

"Certainly Ceolfrith, they have toiled long and hard seeking after perfection and, if you saw the pages I rejected for even the most minor mistake, you would wonder how they managed to complete the task within the time you set my team of scribes." I was determined that my master would understand and appreciate the enormity of the task we had completed. He seemed re-animated by my boldness and replied,

"Bede, I do appreciate the work which has gone into this enterprise and the not inconsiderable input you yourself have made. I presume you have completed three copies of this holy book?" Waiting only momentarily for my nodded assent, he went on. "Take these manuscripts back to Jarrow and have them bound. But do not bind them too heavily, as they need to be transported, so use only a thin skin which will serve as protection for the journey." He stood, eyes unblinking, as if he was mentally checking an itinerary of tasks he had purposed for me to do. "Do you still have the rejected pages?" Once again, almost assuming my nod of assent, he continued with even a greater sense of urgency. "Have these erroneous pages bound too, as if they were a true copy of our great work, so that only you and I would know the difference. Then, listen closely to me Bede, secrete one of the true copies of the book somewhere at Jarrow, known only to you. Do NOT, I emphasise DO NOT, tell anyone where you have hidden it; NOT even me. Then bring me the other three volumes, the two perfect editions and the erroneous one, as soon as you have completed your task. I am in the process of preparing the journey for this most sacred cargo and await only the completion of these items I have assigned you"

Ceolfrith must have noticed my puzzled expression and concern at his animation and before I could form the words of a question he proffered an explanation for his unusual behaviour.

"Bede! There are forces at work which you have no conception of. Forces which would see your work destroyed! Dark forces which recognise the significance of this Codex to the Christian world. This Bible, as I have said my friend, will form the basis for many subsequent translations and will be an important document for the furtherance of the Kingdom of God in this world of sin. Remember, Bede, the words of our dear Christian forebear, Paul of Tarsus. Paul who encountered Jesus personally on that road to Damascus. Blinded by the heavenly light and with the words of our dear saviour Himself ringing in his ears. *"Saul, Saul why do you persecute me?"* Only after he had been directed to Gamelial on Straight Street and, after he repented of his former evil life as persecutor in chief of the members of the Way, did he recover his sight. Did he not write in his letter to the Ephesians, *"for our struggle is not against flesh and blood, but against the rulers, against the authorities, against the powers of this dark world and against the spiritual forces of evil in the heavenly realms."* So my young friend I have tried long and hard to preserve your innocence but now you must be wary of such spiritual wiles of the Antichrist."

Instinctively I sat down, without being invited to by my spiritual senior, in an attempt to recover my thoughts at this intelligence from Ceolfrith. Had my spiritual director lost his senses, had he had some kind of breakdown due to lack of sleep? He had always been so level headed and been a calming influence on the community. Only those who have experienced living in a close knit body of men could understand the tensions it brings. How seemingly trivial things can assume mammoth proportions. Ceolfrith could always handle these clashes of personality and was able to diffuse these disputes with a kind word or even a look. But the man in front of me now was not the calm cool and collected man I knew. Agitated and preoccupied, he had a sense of purpose about his mission which I knew would brook no objection. So, if the situation before us was so important to him, I knew I had to take it seriously. I fixed him with a gaze which I hoped told him he had my full backing and awaited his further instruction.

"I'm sorry if I have alarmed you Bede but I implore you, trust no one with this information I have given you. In fact trust no one! I have tried to protect you, over the years, my friend from the machinations of our community and from the power struggles within our Benedictine Order and the very Church itself. I always wanted you free from such deviations from our true mission as Christians and for you to be free to pursue your scholarship. You have excelled with this Codex and I wish you to concentrate next on your historical works. This country of ours will need to know its roots and where it derives its soul. Our descendants, millennia from now, must know how much their Christian antecedents have shaped their destinies, otherwise they will drown in a void of unbelief. To this end, my son, I hope you will forgive what I must impart to you next."

For the best part of half an hour I have been a mute audience, replying to my interlocutor by means of nods and facial expressions. I have hardly contributed verbally to our conversation, yet my silent attention is sufficient to assure Ceolfrith of my tacit agreement. But what could be so awful a confession so as to elicit my forgiveness? Some heinous crime? Some hidden fault? Whatever the transgression I resolved to forgive my friend and confidante not just this required time but, as the Lord Jesus' exhortation requires, seventy seven times seven.

"When you return those volumes to me, so tenderly bound, it is my sacred duty to deliver one of them to His Holiness Pope Gregory the Second in

Rome. From there the great Church's power will be used to disseminate your work throughout the world. All those dark forces which desire to prevent this happening will try their best to thwart us at every turn. I have a strange foreboding about this journey, an uneasiness I have never felt before." His usual rich and confident voice began to falter at this point but closing his eyes he stole himself for the next declaration. "Therefore I am resigning as abbot of our community and I will leave a letter, to be opened a week after I depart for Rome, appointing Father Prior Hwaetberht as my successor. He is skilled in the ways of managing the community. Wilfred's influence in 'poaching' some of our community for his Hexham venture has been unsettling. You must stay out of the intrigue and infighting which will ensue from my announcement and concentrate on your studies and work." Fatigued by his lack of sleep he wound himself up for one final exhortation. "Bede, I regard you as more than a confrère monk. I regard you as a true brother in Christ and I urge you to accede to the letter of my requests. This is for the benefit of our community, the Church and yourself."

Ceolfrith collapsed into his chair in relief at having disclosed his intentions and immediately I knelt in front of him in humble protestation of his shocking disclosures. He assured me his mind and will were fixed on this course of action and my obedience, as the sole owner of this information, was required. He reminded me once again succinctly of his wishes, namely to return to Jarrow, bind all three copies of the Codex plus the rejected scripts, hide one copy at Jarrow (known only to me) and return the other two copies and bound erroneous copy to him. He then informed me he would hide another copy at Monkwearmouth (known only to him) and take the third copy to Rome. The bound copy of the error strewn parchments would be held in the Monkwearmouth library for reference purposes only. I somewhat reluctantly but obediently concurred with his wishes and was dismissed from his presence.

I am sad to say that this would be the last day I was to see him alive! My mentor, my friend and my one true brother in Christ Jesus would never return to his beloved Northumbria and his spiritual home again. I returned to Jarrow the following day to begin the implementation of his instructions.

Chapter Four
Jarrow

Both Monkwearmouth and Jarrow are extremely important to me. I am unsure of my specific place of birth. All my father would ever tell me was that I was born on monastery land and that he knew that I always belonged to them and that I was destined to be a monk. Even to his dying day, some ten summers ago now, my father Edwin would not disclose the precise location of my entry to this world. As I write these words, my tears are mixed with the ink as I remember my loving father and, as the sad solution dries upon the pages, they will forever bear testament to my heart's grief. But, as St Paul tells us, we must not grieve as those who have no hope grieve. He is not reproving us for grieving for our loved ones but encouraging us to have hope in our soul that we will be reunited with them at that heavenly banquet. It is a hope lost on my mother who still has not accepted her widowhood. It is true that she finds delight in my sibling's children, her own grandchildren and my nieces and nephews. But a large part of her is missing. That missing part is her helpmate and her soulmate; Edwin, her husband and my father. May the angels and saints welcome him into paradise.

If I can paraphrase the words of the prophet Jeremiah, death did indeed climb in through our windows and entered our fortresses and removed the children from our streets and the young men from our public squares. It was in the form of that evil plague which devastated our young men and older ones too. Men of God, dedicated to the Christian cause and yet cruelly cut down in their prime and yes some even past their prime. Containing the disease to within our monastery of Jarrow (thankfully none of the neighbouring populace died) was up to Ceolfrith, Godric and me, a callow youth of nineteen summers. It was up to us to build up the community again. The disease was traced to the monastery's water supply and, once that was isolated, the plague was brought under control. However not before it had wrought its indiscriminate toll on our number.

Volunteers were asked for from Monkwearmouth and, if people thought our decimation was some kind of judgement from God, then the influx of new vocations and new blood must therefore be part of His blessing. We have never known before or since such an outpouring of the Holy Spirit upon our community. Not only were there numbers added to our contingent every day but the quality of those new recruits was beyond compare. Such holy and dedicated young men, so willing to learn from such inadequate a teacher as myself. It was humbling to see the verve and application they gave to their duties and to the Lord. Soon our numbers at Jarrow had swelled and the whole monastery was resounding again to the glory and praise of the Lord.

And so Jarrow grew both in number and repute to be acknowledged as both a place of Godly peace and learning. If Monkwearmouth was the heartbeat of our community, generating energy and power, then Jarrow was the soul of our community, examining its direction and purpose. Monkwearmouth generated the resources in order to enable Jarrow time to think, reflect and advise. A symbiotic relationship, which could only prosper both houses. It is to Ceolfrith that credit for this must be given, for it was under his tutelage that this took place. Ruling with a firm but fair hand he allowed us to flourish but, like a loving father, he was not afraid to admonish his brothers in love. He would celebrate excellence and acknowledge the genuine and invaluable efforts of the mundane.

However he never tolerated mediocrity and challenged us to reach for greater heights in whatever activity we attempted, whether this be spiritual or physical. I speak of his leadership in the past tense as I try to come to terms with his decision to resign his abbatial duties. The responsibilities of the Codex have weighed heavily upon him and I didn't realise how heavily until a few days ago. I am, though, glad of his choice as his successor. Whenever an opportunity as this arises, usually on the death of an abbot or his resignation for ill health or age, there ensues a power struggle with various factions vying for the top post.

Such a struggle took place on Ceolfrith's accession, with previously hidden enmities rising to the surface and the revealed divisions continuing after his appointment. It may seem incongruous to the lay person that these power plays should be in evidence among so holy a band of brothers. But we are only human and our society can be reflective of your society too. Not everyone has such pure motives and ambition is a strong motivating force. Personalities clash and people seek their own positions. Whereas most lay people can choose who to spend their lives with we, as religious, do not have that prerogative. Such was Ceolfrith's ability to heal and unite, that this atmosphere of disunity soon dissipated and we enjoyed an almost idyllic period when we went from strength to strength as a Godly community. He must feel that with his future prolonged absence from the monastery on Codex business in Rome and with the rise of the disruptive Hexham element, there is need of strong leadership with authority the post of abbot brings. I thank God that man is Hwaetberht and not me!

It was not such an outlandish concept of my candidature as abbot as you may think. I do have a certain 'reputation' and I had heard the rumours touting me as a future leader but I have no such aspirations of self promotion. I am grateful to my friend Ceolfrith's insight into my strengths and weaknesses. I know my strength is not leadership but scholarship. It is not administration but the implementation of a holy plan, that is of interest to me. I seek to educate and to facilitate my colleagues. I am not a strong leader but a recogniser and loyal supporter of strong leadership. For the moment I must keep my own council about Ceolfrith's plans but when they are announced I will be Hwaetberht's most loyal and staunch supporter. As the sole recipient of my dear friend's confidence I must also feign surprise when the news is imparted to our community by Hwaetberht. For I am thankful to the Lord Jesus Christ and my dear friend Ceolfrith that I am to be spared the responsibility of high office in order to concentrate on my historical studies.

Before I tell you a little about those studies, perhaps now would be a good time to appraise you of some of the important events in my life since you last heard from me. I couldn't possibly account for ever detail of some twenty summers or more but you may be interested in a few salient points. I think you left me at the point of my first profession as a monk and four summers later, at the age of nineteen, I was ordained a deacon and took my final profession as a monk. This was somewhat early, as the usual age for such commitment was twenty five, and the ceremony was performed by John, Bishop of Hexham. Once again my family and a host of friends were present to witness my ordination into the diaconate. Alas my father never lived to see my ordination to the priesthood when I was aged thirty. He would have been so proud to have participated in a Eucharist where I was the main celebrant. I do though remember his words of advice years before I became a priest. He said I should never forget that all those who participate in the Eucharist, male or female, are priests. All Christians belong to the priesthood of believers and that, during the ceremony, we delegate responsibility, to act on our behalf, to the priest who is officiating at the Eucharist. When he utters those sacred words that Jesus spoke at that Last Supper, *"This is my body broken for you, this is my blood, the blood of the new and everlasting covenant shed for you. Take and eat! Take and drink! For my body is real food and my blood is real drink. Do this in memory of me"* we too, by our presence and accord, invoke the power of the Holy Spirit to change those ordinary items of bread and wine into the body and blood of our Saviour and Lord. I remember this counsel, from my dear departed father, every time I officiate at a Eucharist and invite all those present to say those powerful words with me.

This may seem a controversial idea to some Christians but I base my belief, not on my own thoughts or what I have been taught, but on Holy Scripture itself. I refer to our father in faith Peter, our first Pope and leader of New Testament Christians. In his first letter to his followers he said, *'You also, as living stones, are being built up as a spiritual house, a holy priesthood, to offer up spiritual sacrifices acceptable to God through Jesus Christ. But you are a chosen generation, a royal priesthood, a holy nation, His own special people, that you may proclaim the praises of Him who called you out of darkness into His marvellous light.'* And in that most revealing book of the New Testament, Hebrews, we are told, *'Thus, all Christians are of that holy priesthood and can offer spiritual sacrifices to God. All have the right to go directly to God through Jesus Christ, our High Priest.'* This book shows us how the veil between God and mankind has been torn in two by the blood of Jesus on the Cross. So, we who are unrighteous and unholy are made righteous and holy by His Blood and so are free, male or female, to enter in to the Holy of Holies and encounter the living God personally.

This is my vocation, my calling from God. That calling is to help spread the Gospel or Good News of Salvation for all, be he prince or peasant, man or woman. All are equal before God. All have sinned and fallen short of God's perfect plan. All are in need of a Saviour, someone to stand in the gap created between us and God by our sinfulness. That person is His own dear Son Jesus. As the apostle John (the one whom Jesus loved) put it in his Gospel account, *"For God so loved the world that he gave his one and only Son, that whoever believes in him shall not perish but have eternal life."* For me this short Gospel text encapsulates the whole Bible story in one sentence. It tells me that God is love and He loves the world so much that He gave us what is the most precious thing He has to give: His Son Jesus. It tells us something about our state as sinners; we are in danger of perishing. But God wants ALL to be saved and His Son will die for all those WHO BELIEVE. It is this condition of belief which compels me to do what I do now. For how can anyone believe unless they hear? And how can they hear unless someone tells them? So that is my job. I must do all I can to spread God's word be it here in Jarrow or throughout the world. The simple folk of Jarrow and Northumbria, who are unable to read, will hear the Word of God whilst those erudite people in Europe can read the Word, using my Codex.

Sorry! I should not be so bold as to call it 'my' Codex. I am just an unworthy cog in a great machine which has produced this Codex. Not a noisy, clanking machine belching dirt but a serene room flooded with light and peace. Nevertheless a room of great industry, a room known to us all as the Scriptorium.

Chapter Five
The Scriptorium

The Scriptorium is my favourite room in both monasteries. As I am responsible for this work, I have concentrated my efforts on Jarrow. The Scriptorium at Monkwearmouth is rarely used as I feel the more 'industrial' atmosphere at Monkwearmouth is less conducive to the work which demands a high level of concentration and skill. Also the room itself is not suitable for good scribing. Its aspect is quite dark and light, a crucial requirement of a good Scriptorium, is at a premium at Monkwearmouth.

Therefore a purpose built Scriptorium was designed and constructed for me at Jarrow. Light floods the room from three different aspects; east, south and west, in order to take advantage of the Sun as it moves around the sky during the day. Of course my good friend Brother Gregory at Lindisfarne maintains that the great orange orb does not move an inch! But instead it is we, the Earth, which moves around the Sun. This accounts for the apparent different positions of the Sun during the day and indeed the seasons themselves. Gregory is a passionate scientist and has fallen foul of much of the hierarchy in the Church. He, however, maintains that we should not fear scientific enquiry, as it only ever serves to confirm the greatness of our God. But people become set in their ways and feel threatened by some of the new ideas.

But I digress as my purpose is to tell you about my, sorry, our Scriptorium. Situated handily next to the Library, the Scriptorium is the quiet hub of the monastery. Our founder Benedict, from whom we derive our Benedictine name, instituted a rule, or guide, by which we as monks live. One of his great rules is Ora et Labora which means: prayer and work. This suggests that our day should consist of both aspects so that the two become almost indistinguishable. In Monkwearmouth work consists of many manual tasks such as farming, glass works and building or constructing. We are a much smaller community at Jarrow and have perhaps a more reflective working atmosphere. Perhaps our labora (work) is more cerebral, more intellectual. Nevertheless it is no less important and no less tiring, both physically and mentally. This is the subject of a lot of banter between the monks of the two monasteries, with Jarrow regarded as those 'soft Tynesiders.' Most of it is good natured joshing, though recently there has been more of an edge to the criticism. I feel we take a professional pride in what we do and perhaps feel a little undervalued by the community at times. But the sum of the parts is always greater than those individual contributions and so we learn to thrive as a community of God.

The Rule of St Benedict governs all aspects of our day and the ora (prayer) part of it is strictly laid down for us and you may be interested to see what a typical day looks like from an extract from an old diary, which I kept when I was a newfangled monk and before I was involved with the Scriptorium:

4:50 a.m. I wake up as usual, a little before the rising bell. My body clock has its own alarm, but that doesn't stop me feeling far from fresh. I always have to struggle in the mornings. I take my jug down the dimly lit corridor to the water butt, to fetch water for washing. I then return to my cell and use my washstand and basin. Still not truly awake, I stumble down the main staircase and brave the sharp morning air of the cloister on my way to church. Another day has begun.

5:30 a.m. VIGILS The first service of the day breaks the silent darkness. "Lord, open my lips, and my mouth shall announce your praise." The psalms flow from side to side of the choir, long psalms, telling the story of God's chosen people, telling of the long centuries of watching, of vigil, before the dawning of God's light, of his coming into a world darkened by ignorance, malice and sin.

6:20 a.m. A bowl of milk and a piece of bread, butter and marmalade begins to introduce some life into my still sluggish body. And my mind is clearer by the minute.

7:00 a.m. LAUDS The second service of the day begins as the new born light breaks through the sanctuary windows, and sets the pink and orange bricks ablaze. Praise God, the Creator of Light! Praise Christ, the Son of God, who has risen, Victor over Satan, sin and death! In the words of the canticle, the loving-kindness of the heart of our God has visited us like the dawn from on high.

7:30 a.m. I return to my cell for 'lectio divina', that basic monastic practice of reading the scriptures. I read the scriptures, or rather, I listen to them, trying to catch the voice of the Spirit, who is trying to get through to me, trying to tell me something of how he sees things, of how he wants me to respond to the Father. I can't hear much this morning, but never mind! Sooner or later, the word which is received in quietness will come alive. How often has the memory brought forth the living Word and offered encouragement, correction or a challenge? Lectio divina flows naturally into prayer. Some prefer the church for personal prayer, but I stay in my cell; there are fewer outward distractions. But that does not stop the distractions from within. Waves of thoughts come on, by turns funny and fantastic, foul and fascinating. But they bring me face to face with something of my own darkness and need for God. I try to put myself before Him just as I am; He can cope with all that is within me, even if I cannot. And then deeper, much deeper than all this, I become aware of the roots of my being reaching out, seeking nourishment, seeking a source of stability in the midst of the turbulent void. Mysteriously, a certain confidence is born.

9:00 a.m. TERCE and EUCHARIST The third service of the day, consisting of three short psalms only, is joined with the Eucharist, the very heart of the monastic round. Who can grasp the mystery of Christ's body and blood? We receive the signs, the tokens of his love for us, and we enter into the great mystery of his passion, death and resurrection, to be united with the very source of our salvation. And we go out to share his peace with all around us.

10:00 a.m. After the Eucharist, the monastic day comes down to earth. Today I have been given the job of varnishing the library floor. I move the furniture outside, and sweep the floor, before throwing the windows open, and then rolling the sickly smelling varnish onto the pine boards. A robin hops in through the open door to see what is going on, but he doesn't stay for long. A passer by calls to ask for directions to the Heb Burn and shows interest in my activity. How extraordinary the monastic life seems from the outside, and yet how ordinary from within; just basic human activities, encompassed by faith and prayer.

1:00 p.m. SEXT The fourth service of the day is very short: a hymn, three short psalms, a reading and a prayer. But we are reminded of the Creator when our own affairs are liable to be uppermost in our minds.

1:15 p.m. DINNER We process from the church to the refectory, and after singing grace, we all sit down together. No talking but the reader's heard as we begin our soup. I've never had much difficulty in attending to both my food and the reading, especially if the book being read is an interesting one. Today, it is the poetry of Catullus, an influential Roman poet.

1:45 p.m. After dinner we can relax a little as a community. It is true that the brethren are not always relaxing company; building community is ever one of life's greater challenges. But mostly it is peaceful over a bowl of mead, and today is no exception.

2:20 p.m. NONE The fifth service of the day, like Sext, marks the passing hours, and recalls our minds and hearts to the Creator of time. He fills every moment with his watchful and loving presence. How watchful are we, and how loving?

2:30 p.m. Back to work again. In the laundry this afternoon a small mountain of linen, from kitchen, guest-house and monastic cells, awaits me. The washing is relentless and I am kept busy ironing aprons, napkins and pillow cases using a heavy flat iron I heat on the fire. I like the laundry room; it is an isolated place where few people come, and has a little window overlooking the farmyard and workshops. As the ironing progresses, and I ruminate on the morning's reading, my attention is caught by a sound from outside. I look over to where the two carpenters are hard at work, a man and a young woman. He has worked at Jarrow for many years now, while she has just returned from the birth of her first child. Some people think it's wrong to employ a woman for such work.

4:30 p.m. Afternoon work over, the community meets again, for mead and to talk. But the guest master has no sooner filled his bowl and taken his seat than he jumps up and runs off to receive an unexpected guest. However regular the monastic day may seem, the Spirit is always ready to unsettle us if we start getting too comfortable in our routines.

5:00 p.m. VESPERS The sixth service of the day is an evening sacrifice of praise. We offer to God all we have received in the course of the day, and all we have done, or tried to do with his all powerful help. *"Let my prayer rise like incense before you, O Lord."*

5:30 p.m. After Vespers, I had planned to prepare a class on the liturgy for the novices, but Fr Prior has called a chapter meeting. Class preparation must be postponed until after supper, and I make my way down the steep stone steps to the chapter house. I profess to dislike meetings of every kind, but I have to admit that discussion on matters of common concern does build community. And, just occasionally, my tongue does seem to take delight in keeping the discussion going on and on.

7:00 p.m. SUPPER We sing grace again, we sit down together again, and again we listen to the voice of the reader, first telling of the saints we will commemorate tomorrow, and then reciting a chapter of Saint Benedict's Rule. Finally our minds are taken back to the poetry of Catullus.

8:00 p.m. COMPLINE The seventh and final service of the day, brings the monastic day to its close. *"Now Lord, let your servant depart in peace."* We sing the song of Simeon, the old man, whose life was prolonged by the Lord until his eyes had seen the salvation prepared for all peoples. We give thanks for the mercy we have received today, and pray for a quiet night and a perfect end.

So then! What do you make of my monastic day? Do you think you could cope with it? If you tried it you may be surprised by how ordinary and commonplace our lives are. True we do have to sacrifice many of the things you would hold dear. But we always have a full stomach and we are educated men.

My older sister Gertrude is part of our extended community. She too was schooled by Godric and she accepted holy orders when she was twenty years old. Now she exists as a recluse or hermit nun near Jarrow, at Tyne Dock. She lives a humble and simple life in a small cottage. Mother was not too pleased when she became a nun; she had husbands and children a plenty planned for her. But God had other plans and now I feel mother has grown to accept it. Though I still think she harbours hopes of her renouncing her vocation and marrying a 'nice local boy.' Gertrude is her own woman though and worships here at Jarrow and works with me in the Scriptorium. She is one of my finest scribes and works extremely hard.

This morning the Scriptorium stands empty as I gave all my scribes a day off yesterday after working so hard on our Codex and I asked them to report back after dinner. The tables are strewn with vellum parchments the scribes are currently working on. I am not too happy about this as, in their haste to make the most of their time off, some of the monks have failed to clear up and I am concerned that the sun will fade some of the work they have completed. So, I set to and accomplish what they have neglected, rolling up parchments and neatly filing them carefully in wooden units fixed to the walls. The scribing tables are not set out neatly in rows but at every possible angle in order to take advantage of the light. Long and short candle sticks with various levels of melted wax litter the room. I prefer daylight working as I feel we do our best work then. But when we are pressing on to complete the task, or on dull days, then light is enhanced by use of candle light.

After completing my filing duties I unpack the satchels Mika and I have brought back from Monkwearmouth with the remnants of the Codex I had taken to Ceolfrith for approval. I gently place them in biblical order with their holy partners, ready to be bound together for their long journey to Rome.

Although I have enthused about my Jarrow home I am nevertheless grateful to Monkwearmouth for providing the raw materials needed to produce our literary work. The numerous head of cattle they have provides me with the vellum needed to write upon. Vellum is prepared animal skin or "membrane" used as a material for writing on. The term is derived from the Latin word vitulinum meaning "made from calf." Calf is the young of the animal and sometimes I feel uncomfortable at ill using such a beast. But the best quality vellum is made this way and I believe only the best is good enough for God.

Vellum is generally smooth and durable, although there are great variations depending on preparation and the quality of the skin. The manufacture involves the cleaning, bleaching, stretching on a frame (herse), and scraping of the skin with a crescent-shaped knife (lunarium or lunellum as in luna meaning moon). To create tension, scraping is alternated with wetting and drying.

A final finish may be achieved by abrading the surface with pumice, and treating with a preparation of lime or chalk to make it accept writing or printing ink. Once the skin is completely dry, it is thoroughly cleaned and processed into sheets. The number of sheets extracted from the piece of skin depends on the size of the skin and the given dimensions requested by the order. For example, the average calf skin can provide three and half medium sheets of writing material. This can be doubled when it is folded into two conjoint leaves, also known as a bi-folium.

Once the vellum is prepared, usually a quire is formed of a group of several sheets. This quire is a batch of twenty sheets and is the scribe's basic writing unit. We then make guidelines on the membrane so that writing is level and even. We make small holes in a sheet of parchment in preparation for ruling; this is known to us as pricking. We then rule between the prick marks horizontally and enter our text along those lines.

We also rule vertically to mark the left and right boundary lines for our text.

The type of script we use is called unical. This has been passed down to us from the Romans but I think it was also used by the ancient Greeks too. It is a very beautiful form of handwriting and is difficult to master. It is characterised by broad single stroke letters using simple round forms taking advantage of the new parchment and vellum surfaces, as opposed to the angular, multiple stroke letters, which are more suited for rougher surfaces, such as papyrus as used by the Egyptians. The unical characters have become ever more complex and we exaggerate the ascending and descending letters and my sister Gertrude excels at unical script as well as the preparation of vellum and is in the process of passing on her skills to the other scribes. Although I can not prove it, I believe she has inherited some of these skills from the common sense practical knowledge of our own mother.

I can tell by the chatter noise and laughter that from outside the room that my scribes are returning to their duties. When they settle I upbraided them gently for leaving the Scriptorium in such a messy state. I could tell from their confused looks that my reprimand had fallen on deaf ears. Perhaps I should not have tidied up for them and my chiding would have been backed up with visual evidence as confirmation.

"Now then lady and gentlemen. I am pleased to report that Father Abbot Ceolfrith is very pleased with your work. He has given me the go ahead to have the volumes bound." I couldn't continue my directions because of the cheering and whooping from all concerned. I raised my hand for order and continued. "He even values your erroneous work so much that he has asked me to have that bound too. It will be kept in Monkwearmouth monastery library for reference purposes." This intelligence was met with less enthusiasm from my audience. There were a few moans and groans and whistles as they complained under their breath about my perfectionist approach. Apparently this confirmed their thoughts that the work they had completed was worthy of inclusion and I had perhaps given them much unnecessary extra work.

I ignored their implicit protestations and explained how Ceolfrith wanted a relatively light binding in order to facilitate transportation. To protect the fragile and expensive manuscripts, thick wooden coverings were first devised. These coverings were simply two thick slabs of wood or bark between which the vellum sheets were sandwiched. This is where we get the name codex from which we use for our volumes. It comes from the Latin caudex, which means tree trunk. The slabs of wood thickness was next reduced, and the thinner boards attached, first to one another and later to the vellum sheets as well. This technique afforded not only excellent protection, but if properly executed allowed the book to lie flat when closed, yet permitted the pages to fall open in a graceful arc when opened.

Coverings then began to be made from cloth, leather, precious metals, gems, ivory, and any of a number of further materials. Innovations such as endpapers, leather joints, split boards, French joints, and so on have continually improved the bookbinder's art. It is not presumptuous of me to say that, I believe, Jarrow is one of the best, if not the best, exponents of the binding process. It is one of these lighter leather bindings, that I explain to my cohort, we will be using for these treasured volumes.

So, for the following week our Scriptorium endeavour is solely involved in the binding of these three perfect copies together with the error strewn volume. Stored leather is copiously inspected and selected and then stretched and cut to fit the volumes which are then pressed for a few days to complete the process. All the while our labour is punctuated by the daily routine of the Benedictine day. Gertrude is allowed to stay in a cell set aside for guests to avoid the commute from her cottage. The innovative strides in gender equality, made by Hilda at Whitby, have not been replicated here at Jarrow and I am afraid my sister resides here under sufferance, rather than a woman in her own right. Nevertheless I am grateful for this small concession in order to ensure her freshness for work.

Finally our work is done and the volumes sit proud and identical on the scribe tables in our Scriptorium. I instruct my pupils to pack two copies of the perfect editions together with the faulted one, ready for delivery to Ceolfrith. I order the other copy to be taken to my cell. I offer no explanation or answer to their unspoken questions for this action. I also send a message to Joseph to be ready, with his cart, first thing the morrow morning. Having dismissed my group of workers for the day I slump down into a comfortable carver chair and sit exhausted contemplating our achievements.

This work has been all consuming and I have to put some of my other works on the back burner. My major tome is Historia Ecclesiastica Genti Anglorum or the An Ecclesiastical History of the English People in which I hope to show the growth of the united church throughout England. To this end I want to show how this unity has been achieved by the power of the Holy Spirit despite the disparate kingdoms which have existed. I am also concerned with the concept of time and the age of the world. Connected with this is how we calculate the date of the most important feast in our Church: Easter! As I reflect on my forthcoming travails I am woken from my reverie by a monk bearing a missive from Wilfred at Hexham which demanded my immediate attention and reply. The letter contained an urgent request for me to attend a supper he was giving for the benefit of local dignitaries.

Intrigued by the urgency of his request I returned my acceptance which then was despatched with the courier from Hexham who made off forthwith.

Chapter Six
To hexham

One of my dear friends, Joseph, is employed by the joint monasteries in various roles. Although he had benefited, like Odin and me, from Godric's tutelage he has not pursued an academic career. Such opportunities are not available to those not engaged in a religious vocation and Joseph was too interested in the wiles of the opposite sex to follow my path. He played the field to his heart's content, until he settled down with his one true love, a beautiful girl called Thea, who moved to the area from Cumbria. Her parents were driven out by border raiders and so moved across the Pennines. Joseph became besotted with Thea who, knowing his reputation with the ladies, made him work hard to woo her. Now they are settled with their three children at Primrose, just a mile up stream from me at Jarrow. Odin too lives close by and they both eke out a living on their respective small holdings, as well as gaining useful employment from the twin monasteries. We have though, remained firm friends and I was proud to have officiated at their marriages as well as baptising their children. Their wives are pillars of the local Christian community, helping those less blessed than they are. I spend much time with both Odin and Joseph's families and I am pleased to say they have adopted my mother as a sort of surrogate grandmother.

Today Joseph has been employed to take the two bound copies of the Codex plus the similarly bound copy of the reject parchments. Only an expert could detect the difference between the perfect editions and the erroneous edition. Only a perfectionist like myself or Ceolfrith or indeed my team of scribes in the Scriptorium could tell them apart. I feel a little guilty, as the volumes are loaded on to the cart that will bear these holy objects with more mundane books of accounts and everyday items such as pots and pans and jugs needed by the mother house. I feel uncomfortable at not accompanying the work on which we have laboured for so long. I feel remorseful at having been so harsh with my brother monks in the Scriptorium, as I am faced with the evidence of my strictness. Although I have added a few blank parchments, as instructed by Ceolfrith, so the erroneous volume resembles the perfect ones in size and weight, nevertheless we could have almost completed a full Codex from the near perfect rejected copies. I understand that adherents to the Islamic faith (they believe in the one true God but not Jesus as His divine Son) who are doing any form of religious task, incorporate a deliberate mistake in their work. This is because they believe that perfection belongs to God alone. But I am afraid I disagree with them as I feel the purpose of these holy volumes is to glorify our God and promote His word in successive centuries, so we should only be satisfied with our best.

"See to it that you take extreme care with your precious cargo, my friend," I said, patting the impatient beast that would pull its unique load. The animal pawed the ground and blew down its nostrils, eager to be underway. "Make sure you get there before nightfall. No stopping off for some ale and crack with your old mates at the inn near Shields." As well as the ladies, Joseph also enjoyed a drink and natter in the company of his male contemporaries. Often Thea would have to send down to the local hostelry and force him to come home for his meal. He was never the worse for drink and in fact used to nurse one pint for most of his time in the ale house. Much to the innkeeper's annoyance!

"Bede! How must you regard me? Do you really think I would be so tardy? Mind you I can well remember the days when we would bunk off Godric's seventeen out of twenty tests for a game of kickbladder. We would play at any opportunity and, as I seem to remember, you were the one who used to suggest it. I haven't had time for a game for years!" Joseph's grin lit up his whole face and, without waiting for a reply, he clicked his tongue for the young pony to begin his journey. The route would see the horse, cart and driver take the riverside cart track from Jarrow to South Shields tracing its way past Arbeia, scene of our Kickbladder Tournament win, then on to the mouth of the river. He would then turn right and follow the coastal track until it met my foot pathway at Bents Cottages. Although the footpath route was much quicker, as it cut across country, the holy volumes were now too heavy to be carried by hand. Only parts of the Codex had ever been transported by hand for Ceolfrith's approval, so this was the first time a full volume had been carried. Although not usually a big problem, the possibility of theft was also reduced by this method and Ceolfrith had been almost paranoid about security. Therefore Joseph was also collecting Odin to ride with him as extra insurance. It was my intention to act as the third 'amigo', as our Spanish brothers say, but Wilfred's, somewhat urgent, invitation has pre-empted this plan. I stood watching and, occasionally, waving until Joseph had disappeared from sight, as if my quiet presence helped secure the enterprise. I was sure, though, that the silent prayer I sent up to heaven would ensure a safe delivery.

I now made to begin my journey of approximately thirty miles to Hexham at the request of my friend and colleague Wilfred. I intend breaking my trip at my sister's house at Heddon where I would spend the night. I asked Wilfred's courier to make a small diversion to prepare my sister for my arrival, when he returned my acceptance to his master. My younger sister Bridget has done rather well for herself, marrying a man of fairly noble stock. He has a sizeable acreage of arable land as well a goodly stock of cattle, sheep and various fowl. He has many serfs whose livelihoods depend upon him. I am pleased that he is a kind master and I have heard only good reports of him. They have both asked my mother to live with them but she has refused, saying that she was born a Heb Burn lass and that she will die a Heb Burn lass. She does though, miss her grandchildren and has decided to travel with me. She will stay with Bridget for a few days whilst I conclude my business with Wilfred and we will return together. Unfortunately, as the cart is in use to transport the Codex, we will have to complete most of the journey on foot, or I will anyway. I hope that this will only be for a short way for my mother, as a friend I know at Felling has a donkey, which he puts at our disposal when he has no use for it. Before leaving I briefed the young novice monks in the Scriptorium as to the progress I hoped to see from them. They weren't too pleased at the news that Gertrude would be in overall charge but I reminded them of their vow of obedience and the need for humility in all things.

So, the first leg of my journey sees me arrive at the old homestead to pick my mother up. I can almost hear her shouting Edwin! Edwin! And then see my father ambling unhurried from whatever activity he was undertaking. I miss him. I miss him dearly. I have travelled the length and breadth of Britain and Europe and have met men and women that one day our great

Church will no doubt elevate to sainthood. Yet, I have yet to meet a more saintly or holy person as my own father. He would never care to be elevated to sainthood, nor would he wish his visage etched into wood and garishly decorated and venerated as a holy icon. But I know that this simple man of God enjoys his place at the heavenly banquet and he will still be humbly serving his Lord and Saviour as he did here on earth.

"Your ears must be burning my lad! I was just talking to my good neighbour Agnes about you. I told her you'd be late! You'll be late for your own funeral, praise be to God not for these many years yet I hope! Not before mine surely? Though I've asked the Creator of the sky and seas to bring that date close. But for my sins He keeps me in this veil of tears, apart from my beloved husband and your dear father." My mother shuffled forward with her bundle of luggage, rehearsing the words I had heard so many times before. Yet, since my father died I had not heard her utter the word which I would love to hear her utter again; his name! She always referred to him as husband or father but never by that name that brought us so much joy and happiness; Edwin!

I made my usual abortive apology and informed her of my plan to improve her mode of transport. She did not disappoint my anticipation of further berating at her perceived aggrievement at being thought too infirm to complete the journey to Heddon on foot. However her relief at the news was also obvious and we completed the second leg of my journey to Felling. As we neared our friend Jacob's small holding she could see the animals corralled and feeding on straw.

"I hope he has one with a placid temperament? I don't want a stubborn one or one that's going to bite!" said mother, her eyes widening in anticipation.

Since I last saw Jacob he had acquired another two beasts and so my mother was now being presented with a choice of animal. Jacob himself was a man who exuded the placidity my mother so desired in one of his donkeys. Of Jewish descent, Jacob converted to Christianity as a young man. Converts to Christianity are usually the most zealous of believers but Jacob, being a cradle Jew, made his conversion all the more powerful. I had heard him, in meetings, witness to his new found faith most vociferously. To him it seemed so obvious that the prophecies of the Old Testament were met in Jesus in the New Testament. He could not understand how unbelievers could not see this for themselves. An otherwise placid and easy going man, could become animated and excited when the topic of conversation came round to faith.

Jacob tenderly took my mother's hand and led her to his favoured beast and before long she was treating it like a dear pet lamb. Satisfied with our choice of donkey, we said our farewells and thanks for the help given to us. Jacob informed me that he may well see me again in Hexham, as Wilfred had invited him to a feast he was giving. Wilfred had taken to inviting many of the Northumbrian worthies and noble land owners to these dinners. They had become quite notorious for the exchange of new ideas about the faith and its progress throughout the country. However there were rumours of debauchery and conduct unbecoming to men of the cloth. Wilfred was very much a man of the world and sought to ingratiate himself with men of influence and power. This had won him as many enemies as friends in the secular and clerical worlds but he maintained he was doing this from the best of motives and for the furtherance of the Gospel.

With the aid of the donkey I could now increase the pace of our progress up the Tyne valley. I never cease to be amazed at the beauty of the Northumbrian countryside and today was no exception. The pink May Blossom and white Apple Blossom trees provided a welcome shade from the unseasonably warm weather. We broke off from our exertions for refreshment, preferring one of the pies my mother prepared to the more prosaic bread and cheese I had brought from Jarrow. This was my staple if unimaginative picnic fare and, although usually quite satisfied with this menu, mother's provision was far more appetising. She informed me that, we were though limited to one of her produce, as the other pies were destined for Bridget's 'bairns', as she called them, who loved her cooking, preferring it to their own mother's! My mother was never slow in promoting her own skills. I think her self consciousness at being intellectually inferior (as she perceived) to her husband and offspring, made her push her own common sense practical abilities. As she was prone to put it, "all your book learning never put a meal on the table."

Duly refreshed we were able to complete our journey to Heddon. On the outskirts of the small village we were greeted by the sight of the crumbling remains of the Roman Emperor Hadrian's wall. Built by Roman soldiers, sent half way across the world to this most northerly and inhospitable outpost, it was meant to halt the hostile Scots and Picts that even the most powerful army on earth could not tame. Latterly, as an uneasy peace replaced the former hostilities, it became more of a customs post, allowing comings and goings across the border at various points along the wall. Since the Romans left Britain the wall has fallen into disrepair, with many inhabitants using the stone to build their own dwellings. I and many other prominent historians have frowned on this practice. We maintain that, from an historical point of view, we should seek to preserve our own history for future generations to learn about us. Like it or not the Romans are part of our history and we should record and preserve as much as possible. Secondly, and perhaps even more relevantly, the Romans have left us with an abundance of quarries from which we can get as much stone as we want. Therefore there is no need to wreck these historic sites. I am glad that my sister's husband Newton has banned any further destruction of the wall at Heddon, as it is situated on his land. The site is so well preserved that the village is becoming known as Heddon on the Wall.

We drop down from the wall to my sister and brother in law's property and laid out in front of us is the sight of the whole Tyne Valley almost to Felling. Dusk is gathering and there is the twinkle of a myriad of homely properties, lighting their rooms as families gather together soon to eat their evening meal. They begin to merge with an horizon of black, interspersed with stars, so that it is impossible to distinguish were land ceases and sky begins. And so we are all enveloped in God's starry love. Bridget is waiting at the door with her baby daughter Ruth in her arms and her son Fenwick at her side. Her husband, alerted by the sheep dog's barking, joins them on the porch and puts a protective arm around his wife. As we draw nearer he breaks his cordon of protection and motions towards us.

"Hilda! Bede! Welcome, good to see you again. Come, give me the donkey and help your mother down." His strong arms gripped the reins of the ass and the beast instinctively responded with unerring obedience. Mother slid down the back of the animal and embraced Newton as if he were her own son. I felt a pang of jealousy at this sight, which I quickly banished from my mind, as I thrust out my hand in welcome response to our host for the evening. Taking it in his hairy right fist he shook mine until I thought my arm might be dislocated from its socket. Newton is a handsome man, six feet tall or more. Although from a well connected Northumbrian family, he was still a man of the land with a physique to match. He would never ask a servant or labourer on his farm to do something which he himself was not capable of. His father had bequeathed him several hundred acres of prime Northumbrian land but Newton had more than improved upon his inheritance by hard work and good management. He calls to a young boy, forking hay in a nearby barn, to come over and greet his grandmother. This is Francis their oldest child. Soon all family members are intermingled, exchanging greetings and kisses and the boy takes the reins of the donkey and escorts it to the barn. He dismantles the bit and bridle and takes the blanket from its back which had been acting as a makeshift saddle. He secures it in a stall and leaves the donkey contentedly munching on its feed and returns to our group.

After much cooing over children and exchange of gossip we adjourn to our rooms where our relations have provided bowls of water for our ablutions, as we prepare for dinner. No need for the modest provisions which we have brought as a joint of ham is quietly roasting in the kitchen. This is quickly devoured by the tired travellers and hungry children. Bridget excuses herself towards the end of the meal to breast feed the baby. Meanwhile Newton and I move to the veranda and drink a little mead to help our digestion. Talk turns to the purpose of my journey which will conclude in Hexham tomorrow. I was surprised at the opinion my brother-in-law offered without any prompting from me.

"I do not wish to speak ill of your friend and colleague Wilfred but I must urge you to have a care in his company tomorrow." Newton nodded his head as if to emphasise his disapproval. "I too have been invited and ordinarily I would not attend. I have done so in the past and I am afraid it was not to my liking." Newton realised he had come too far not to explain further but I could see that he was choosing his words carefully. "The evening started off well enough after we had all attended Vespers in the Abbey. But degenerated later... how can I say... well really it became quite unruly with arguments, drunkenness and raucous behaviour towards the end." Wrongly anticipating embarrassment on my part, his cheeks flushed red and I tried to improve his discomfort by reassuring him that I had already heard the rumours about Wilfred's laissez-faire attitude. Newton continued, "If you will permit me Bede I would like to go with you tomorrow. It is not that I don't think you can look after yourself, I just feel that there is strength in numbers."

Touched by my brother-in-law's concern for me I agreed that we should go together and he suggested that we travel the ten miles or so on horseback. I laughed at this suggestion as four legged quadrupeds and I just do not mix (save for the gentle donkey which had so successfully conveyed my mother) and I had suffered many abortive attempts to learn to ride. In truth if I could only master this task it would make my frequent journeys between our twin monasteries much easier.

However Newton reassured me that I had not learnt at his hands and that he would provide me with such a docile steed that I would be won over to this mode of transport. I reluctantly agreed! Secretly however I hoped that my brother-in-law's tuition would be successful.

After settling the children down to bed Bridget joined her husband, mother and brother around the fire. Although it had been a warm day this had not been replicated after the sun had set and so the welcome crackle of logs burning provided warm comfort on a chilly evening. We began to reminisce about father and, before we became too maudlin, Newton contributed,

"My dear mother in law, I regret not having met your husband Edwin. He seems like he was a great character and a true servant of God." My sister's husband oozed sincerity and concern about not having met my father. I could vouchsafe that Edwin would have approved of Bridget's choice and he would have revelled in helping on their ample homestead.

"Aye! He was that Newton." replied my mother, "And you know what son, I see a lot of him in you. I can see what Bridget sees in you my lad."

For the second time that evening I saw my host flush red with coy embarrassment and to save him further mortification I broke into a favourite hymn of my father's and before too long the house rang with sweet harmonies

Now the green blade rises from the buried grain,
Wheat that in the dark earth many years has lain;
Love lives again, that with the dead has been:
Love is come again, like wheat that springs up green.

In the grave they laid Him, Love Whom we had slain,
Thinking that He'd never wake to life again,
Laid in the earth like grain that sleeps unseen:
Love is come again, like wheat that springs up green.

Up He sprang at Easter, like the risen grain,
He that for three days in the grave had lain;
Up from the dead my risen Lord is seen:
Love is come again, like wheat that springs up green.

When our hearts are saddened, grieving or in pain,
By Your touch You call us back to life again;
Fields of our hearts that dead and bare have been:
Love is come again, like wheat that springs up green.

I had forgotten how beautiful my mother's singing voice was. She had a haunting clarity and tone to her range that transcended the accompaniment of our inadequate vocals. I knew she was not really singing with our three harmonies but with the silent voice of my father. They would often sing this hymn as a duet at home and, like my mother, I was transported in time and distance to our homestead at the Heb Burn. We sat for a few moments in silent reflection, remembering a holy father and husband, all the three family members in quiet accord, with our new in law allowing us the moment of remembrance without need of interjection. We all realised it was time to bed down for the night and so warm embraces and kisses were exchanged as we all retired to our chambers. The embers of the fire smouldered in the grate and continued to heat our dwelling as we all surrendered our spirits to the night and the Lord.

Chapter Seven
Wilfred

I rose before the family, at around five in the morning, to read my Lectio Divina (Divine Office). Perhaps if I can just say a few words about this devotion; it is a traditional Benedictine practice of scriptural reading, meditation and prayer, intended to promote communion with God and to increase the knowledge of God's Word. It does not treat Scripture as texts to be studied, but as the Living Word. The Gospel of John begins with one of my favourite texts, *"In the beginning was the Word and the Word was with God and the Word was God."* I certainly believe when I read those words in my small book that I am encountering the actual Word made flesh. Just as I believe I receive that Word in the form of bread and wine in the Eucharist so I believe I receive Him in the form of velum and ink in the Bible and my Divine Office.

Traditionally, Lectio Divina has four separate steps: read, meditate, pray and contemplate. First a passage of Scripture is read, then its meaning is reflected upon. This is followed by prayer and contemplation on the Word of God. The focus of Lectio Divina is not a theological analysis of biblical passages but viewing them with Christ as the key to their meaning. For example, given Jesus' statement in John 14:27: *'Peace I leave with you; my peace I give unto you'*, an analytical approach would focus on the reason for the statement during the Last Supper, the biblical context, etc. In Lectio Divina, however, the practitioner enters and shares the peace of Christ rather than dissecting it. In some Christian teachings, this form of meditative prayer leads to an increased knowledge of Christ. Sometimes after completing my reading I will return to a phrase or even a word and I will meditate upon this for a few minutes. I can not begin to tell you what revelations I have received during these holy times.

Today, I am afraid, is not one of those days of divine revelation, as I am interrupted in my devotions by my young nephew Fenwick who has an abundance of questions about my daily prayer life. I answer his questions as best I can and he leaves me nonplussed to collect some fresh water for our breakfast from a nearby well. Soon I am called to the table where there is such an abundance that I feel I am fed for the whole day from my sibling's generosity. Her husband advises me that, as we have plenty of time to make our journey to Hexham, he will spend the morning teaching me the rudiments of horsemanship, assuring me that he has earmarked a particularly agreeable horse for the purpose. This animal had been christened Buttercup by my sister but my initial reassurance quickly dissipated as I struggled to master even the most basic skills.

Much to the amusement of my family, who seemed to have nothing better to do than watch my endeavours, the horse decided to go in totally the opposite direction to which it had been instructed. At one point it bolted across the field, putting me in fear of my very existence. Thankfully Newton, an accomplished horseman, was ready mounted and galloped to the rescue, managing to grasp the reins and bring the beast to a halt. My protestations proved fruitless and Newton persisted with his instructions, building my confidence with praise for even the most minute progress I made. After what seemed like an eternity (lasting only an hour) the pupil had become the master of the young animal. I was able to make Buttercup do my bidding and I was declared competent enough to commence the last part of the journey which I had begun yesterday.

I must say that sitting on top of the horse I felt master of all the Northumbrian countryside that I surveyed. We passed the time in idle chit chat about Newton's farming activities, with occasional information returned about events at Jarrow and Monkwearmouth. Newton was intrigued by my work on the Codex and surprisingly asked quite pertinent questions about it. I was impressed by his knowledge of scripture and monastic life. As we approached the town of Corstopitum, where the Roman settlement was being sacked by Wilfred's men, we were accosted by a man known to Newton.

"Good sire, my Lord Newton, I must humbly impinge upon your travels to request a word with your holy companion." Newton told the man that we had urgent business at the Abbey in Hexham and that we were anxious to arrive before nightfall. However the man would not be assuaged by Newton's dismissal but instead addressed his comments directly to me. "Holy friar I know you to be that son of God and son of Jarrow – Bede! Truly a venerable personage, known abroad and in this desolate county. I know you to be a man blessed by God and well versed in the healing ministry. I implore you to divert your animals and come to my homestead where my mother-in-law, the beloved mother of my own dear wife, lies sick and in mortal danger." The man gasped for breath after delivering his soliloquy and I could see that his determination would not be easily turned aside. I chose my reply carefully.

"Sir! I must correct you in that I am a brother of the Benedictine Order and not a friar and I must also inform you that I have no power whatsoever to heal your relative. For I am only a man like yourself. But all things are possible to him who believes" My words seemed to spur my interlocutor on to speak out even more confidently as he said,

"I believe, holy brother Bede, that it is by the power of Our Lord Jesus Christ that my wife's tender mother can be healed. But, like that faithful father in the Gospel, I cry out to the Lord to help my unbelief"

"You have answered well, good and faithful servant," I said, dismounting from my horse. "Lead on to your home and let us see what can do done. I do not think that this will end in death." The man beckoned us on to a small cottage where his family were found to be anxiously awaiting the help that the head of the house had been seeking. Newton waited outside with the steeds whilst I entered.

The sick woman was not much older than me, perhaps only in her late forties, and lay on a rudely constructed bier, a blanket covering her body with only her sallow faced head peering over it. In truth she seemed near to death and her breathing was low and shallow. I took a small phial containing holy oil from a pocket within my tunic and traced the sign of the cross on her forehead.

"Just as our father in faith Peter's mother-in-law lay sick in the Gospel of Mark, so as Our Lord Jesus did, I also order this sickness to be gone. This I command in the name of the Lord Jesus Christ. Be gone. Sister receive your healing" The assembled family and I waited in silence, as nothing appeared to happen. They looked anxiously at me and I raised my left hand to pre-empt any questions they were thinking of making. Then, before our eyes her colour appeared to improve, then a cough and her eyelids, previously tightly closed, flickered and then opened. She sat up in bed looking quizzically at us, as if to enquire about our presence there at her bedside. Then uncannily, like Peter's mother-in-law in the Bible, she rose and asked what our requirements were. The whole family erupted in grateful celebration as she disclaimed all the fuss they were making. Her son-in-law and daughter thanked me profusely and I had to remind them that it was not I who had healed her but it was by the grace of Almighty God. I had to decline their offer of hospitality, as this diversion had delayed our journey to Hexham, and with their thanks and praise ringing in our ears we set off to meet with our host Wilfred. I could see that Newton was a little perturbed by these happenings and asked me,

"Bede, you said you had no power to heal, yet what has just happened in that humble dwelling?"

"I assure you my dear brother that indeed I have no power to heal so much as a pimple." I could see that my protestation did nothing to convince my companion. "Nor is it some kind of magic or sophistry. No, it is the power of God to heal and that power is available to all believers, great or low born. It is all there in the Word of God, the Bible, and I wish that all men could have the same access to it as I have. It is my sincere wish to complete a translation in the vernacular, in the language of the people. This is something I have against the Church. My scribes and I have just completed the great Codex at the request of the Pope. I understand that Latin is the lingua franca or the language most commonly used in Europe and it is appropriate that the Codex should be written so. But I believe for the power of the Bible to be disseminated throughout the world, then translations should also be made in the individual country's tongue. So I wish to see French bibles, German bibles and English bibles. This will

54

then enable all brothers and sisters in Christ throughout the world to avail themselves of the eternal verities of our faith." I felt as if I was on a bit of a rant and so stopped abruptly and waited the reaction of my brother-in-law to my diatribe.

This answer seemed to satisfy his curiosity and we travelled on in silence for the rest of the journey. This is, I am afraid, yet another controversial belief I hold and my wish that all believers have the same access to the scriptures, as we learned students do, is not popular amongst my superiors and confrères.

We arrived at Hexham at around four in the afternoon and the guest master directed us to a guest house adjacent to the Abbey, which was very much a work progressing well towards completion. Scaffolding was still propped up against incomplete walls and stones strewn on the ground. Our horses were taken from us for stabling by a stable lad. After depositing what luggage we'd brought, we were then taken to a common room where the monks and guests were meeting in advance of the service of Vespers, which would then be followed by the evening meal. Wilfred had constructed the accommodation and refectory first and was now using this base to concentrate his efforts on finishing the building work. The abbey chapel was now virtually complete and water tight with just the walls of a few ante rooms to be constructed and then roofed.

Newton was familiar with a number of the land owners who had been invited and began to converse easily with them. Although treated with all politeness, I found a number of the monks who had assembled rather aloof and unfriendly towards me, especially the contingent who I knew from their time at Monkwearmouth. Some of them had made the transfer to Hexham and were now permanently assigned to this community and others were here only on temporary secondment, in order to assist with the building work and to help establish the Abbey. I was glad to see the friendly face of Jacob and was able to make small talk with him. Wilfred was noticeable by his absence though in all honesty I appreciated the demands of leading a community and I did not expect a personal welcome from him. After receiving some light refreshment and discussion with a few junior monks we were ready for the service of Vespers. Only the monks processed to the nave of the church, with Wilfred presiding, whilst the guests assembled in the pews at the back of the church.

Vespers is a poignant service and one in which we are able to rejoice in the accomplishments of the day, yet acknowledge our poverty of spirit before God as we glorify Him. As the sun sets to the west of the town its rays dance playfully across the altar and the assembled priests and brothers bow low in reverent acknowledgement.

The introductory prayer declares in Latin:

> O God, come to our aid.
> O Lord, make haste to help us.
> Glory be to the Father and to the Son
> and to the Holy Spirit,
> as it was in the beginning,
> is now, and ever shall be,
> world without end.
> Amen. Alleluia.

We then sing our plain chant hymns and psalms, one of which was particularly apt bearing in mind the distinguished noble guests who had been invited to dinner by Wilfred:

> Preserve me, Lord,
> I put my hope in you.
> I have said to the Lord
> "You are my Lord,
> in you alone is all my good."
> As for the holy and noble men of the land,
> in them is all my delight.
> But for those who run to alien gods,
> their sorrows are many.
> I will not share in their libations of blood.
> I will not speak their names.

More canticles, and psalms are sung before the service concludes and the body of monks leave the church and process to the refectory for supper. The guests are then invited by a junior monk to join the body of monks and directed to a guest table. I am situated on the top table with Wilfred and Father Prior. I can see my brother-in-law Newton standing in his position on the guest table awaiting the Grace Before Meals said by Father Prior. At the amen there is much noise, as the assembly take their positions and await their meal served by those monks who have been deputed to do so. The Rule of St. Benedict instructs that meal time should be in silence, save for the voice of the reader who would remind us of our founder's rules or some other spiritual text. This was largely adhered to by the assembled monks and guests, during the reading from the book of Habakkuk, and it was only when this reading had been completed that the behaviour of some monks deteriorated.

As well as an abundance of meat and vegetables, copious amounts of mead and wine were offered to the diners. Most respectfully declined any excess of either but a small contingent of monks ate and drank excessively. It was common knowledge that Wilfred allowed discourse amongst the monks during the evening meal contrary to St. Benedict's advice and rule. Inevitably the drink had a loosening affect on their tongues and self restraint and a hubbub of deep male voices arose. The exact details of their clandestine conversations were known only to the parties involved and the rumble of noise exploded into raucous laughter and guffaws. This disturbance grew to a crescendo when one of the group slapped his hand on the table as if in emphasis of a particular point. Simultaneously glances were thrown across the room in my direction and I had the distinct feeling that I was the object of their mirth. One of the group could be clearly seen to be egged on by his peers and indeed he rose to his feet and, with a noticeable sway in his stance, addressed his comments to me.

"Brother Bede it is good to see you out of your den of comfort at Jarrow where you enjoy the protection of Abbot Ceolfrith." suppressing a belch and seeing that Wilfred had not intervened he continued with more gusto, "However now that the good Lord Abbot has departed for mother Rome perhaps you would now have the courage to defend your views before us this night. May I be so bold as to say your ….heretical views!." This last comment was applauded by the speaker's co-conspirators with loud whoops of agreement and banging of tables. Unaccustomed as I was to such unorthodox behaviour, I could only sit and accept his criticism. I caught sight of Newton, on the junior guest table at the back of the room, motion with his right hand as if to say, stay calm and do nothing. Before I had any opportunity to respond a fellow monk from Monkwearmouth, called Sixtus, joined in the fray.

"I think my learned brother is referring to your outlandish ideas about the age of the world and also your obsessive fixation with the calculation of the date of Easter, to say nothing of the so called miracles attributed to your intervention. If you want my opinion...." he said to the accompaniment of here heres and more banging on tables.

Before he could give me the benefit of his no doubt unflattering opinion, Brother Chad, an Irish monk who had arrived with his brother Ced to help Wilfred establish the Abbey at Hexham, stood up with his finger to his mouth. Sixtus, not yet drunk enough to challenge the authority of Chad, reluctantly gave way to the more senior monk. Chad waited in that same attitude until all the recalcitrant monks realised he wished to address the assembly. Like naughty schoolchildren the noise gradually subsided as the silent call to order dawned on them. Not until he had the full attention of everyone did he venture to speak.

"You know my dear brothers the very first word of the rule of our own dear Benedict is.....'Listen!'" Immediately the whole assembled throng were held in thrall to the speaker's innate aura of authority. Surveying the room and making eye contact with the offending monks he continued, "If my memory serves me right, the first sentence of the Prologue reads, *'Listen, O my son, to the precepts of thy master, and incline the ear of thy heart, and cheerfully receive and faithfully execute the admonitions of thy loving Father, that by the toil of obedience thou mayest return to Him from whom by the sloth of disobedience thou hast gone away.'* I am afraid dear brothers the sloth of your disobedience is made manifest in your behaviour tonight. It is with a heavy heart that I must admonish you and call you back to the very basis of our existence. I implore you to moderate your behaviour and reflect upon the rule you first subjected yourself to" Chad's words had a sobering effect on the misbehaving monks and they visibly cowered under the gentle but firm criticism.

He pointed out to them that he doubted if they had even read any of my treatise. He then suggested that, if I was agreeable, I could give a series of lectures over the next week expounding my views. The brothers would have the opportunity to question my proposals but this would be done in a respectful and Christian way. He concluded that all brothers should rededicate their vocations and that the Rule of Benedict be exemplified more prominently at meal times and study times. (As it should have been) All the while Wilfred sat as an interested yet passive observer. His face set as stone, expressionless yet betraying an inner turmoil at the evening's events. What was left of the meal was completed in total silence and there followed a noticeably more prayerful and thoughtful service of Compline.

So, over the next five days I was able to set forth my theories and refute the charges of heresy made against me. Newton returned to his home to tell my mother that our departure would be delayed. We agreed that she would not object to more time spent with her daughter and grandchildren.

I do not propose to rehearse my full arguments here but the sticking points were, I feel, successfully addressed by reference to my work On the Reckoning of Time (De Temporum Ratione) and I commend it to you when I fully complete it. In my lecture I was able to use my research to demonstrate the ancient and current view of the cosmos to my listeners. I think they were surprised by my knowledge of science, as I explained how the spherical earth influenced the changing length of daylight and how the seasonal motion of the Sun and Moon influenced the changing appearance of the New Moon at evening twilight. I also explained the relationship between the changes of the tides at a given place and the daily motion of the Moon. The interest in this subject arose when I was a boy and when I met Brother Gregory on Lindisfarne. From these studies I was able to devise a way of computing the date of Easter.

I was also able to go on and explain my ideas about the age of the world. Once again using my research rather than the previously accepted authority of Isidore of Revile, I calculated that Christ had been born nearly four thousand years after the creation of the world rather than the five thousand years previously believed. Once I had laid my findings before my confrères they were able to appreciate my viewpoint even if not all of them agreed with me. At the close of my lectures I was heartened by my former adversary's words as Sixtus rose and said,

"My dear brother Bede, I stand before you a chastened man and wish to offer you profuse and profound apologies. I thank you for your cogent and well informed arguments and you now have the admiration, if not the agreement, of your brothers." Chad and his brother Ced then led us in prayers of thanksgiving and as the meeting broke up I was congratulated personally by many of my former enemies.

I took the opportunity of a few moments of freedom to visit the crypt of the Abbey. The cold Northumbrian stone, stolen from the old Roman fort at Corstopitum, hemmed me in, womb like and tomb like. Nevertheless it is a holy space where you can be alone with your thoughts and explore your spirituality. Before I know it an hour has disappeared and I am interrupted by a young messenger who requests that I attend on his Abbot Wilfred as soon as possible. I concur and ascend the steep steps which bring me up to the middle of the nave and I follow the lad to Wilfred's office.

"Bede! My old friend, how I have neglected your presence this week but I am pleased that the bad feeling of your first evening has been resolved. I am grateful for the ministrations of Chad and Ced. They have become stalwarts of my administration."

I felt duty bound to express my misgivings at the rather cavalier attitude he had towards the Rule of St. Benedict which had led to the chaotic events. He reassured me that the two aforementioned brothers had implemented a more stringent adherence to the Rule and he would have a greater reverence for it in the future. He admitted that his desire to ingratiate himself with the nobility had caused him to lose focus. I feel we have now cleared the air between us and we can resume our friendship. Before leaving Hexham, Wilfred had some important information to impart to me.

"I have received a communication from Monkwearmouth. Hwaetberht has called a convocation in seven days time, allowing for those brothers here and in other postings to return to your mother house for the meeting." I felt myself flush red at this news and Wilfred was not slow to pick up on it. "I see by your reaction that you have some prior knowledge as to what this is about. I will not embarrass you further as to the reason for this sudden call and suggest that you make plans to leave as soon as possible."

Chapter Eight
The Codex Sets Forth For Rome

It was the day after Joseph and Odin had delivered the three volumes, the two perfect and one imperfect, that Ceolfrith set off for Rome in order to present them to His Holiness Pope Gregory the Second. He had everything in place for his departure and awaited only the Codex cargo from Bede's friends, which was to be the sole purpose of his visit to the eternal city. The responsibility of his mission weighed heavily upon his heart and the sense of foreboding was palpable. Perhaps only Ceolfrith, and possibly Bede, realised the full significance of this pandect work. It contains the full body of the Word of God based on Jerome's work and as such will be an indispensable tool to all Bible scholars in the future. Ceolfrith believed the very furtherance of the Gospel was dependent upon this work and so he regarded this journey to Rome as the most important one of the many he'd undertaken over the years. He was conscious, though, that not everyone shared his excitement at the prospect of this Codex forming the basis of faith for future generations. He had warned his young brother monk about the sinister forces abroad but he was unsure if Bede had realised the true extent of the danger. Ceolfrith was, though, glad that Bede had fulfilled his urgent request to secrete the third copy of the Codex at Jarrow, and, as he had been advised, had not disclosed the whereabouts of the volume to anyone. Ceolfrith could begin his travels happy in the knowledge that whatever happened to him on the journey, he had at least one copy of the Codex back at home to fall back on.

There was one other thing that weighed heavily upon Ceolfrith's mind and that was his role as abbot and leader of the Monkwearmouth and Jarrow communities. He had no second thoughts about his decision to relinquish his position and had only confided this information to Bede. He had written his letter of resignation and had ordered his missive not to be opened until five days after his departure. In the letter he also asked for Hwaetberht to call a convocation of the community to announce his decision to resign and his wishes as to who his successor should be. All monks currently on business in other houses were to be called back to discuss this momentous decision. It was not necessarily a given that the community would accede to his wish that Hwaetberht succeed him but he hoped the forceful language used in his letter would persuade them.

Only a small party of Ceolfrith, Captain Jean, Tomas and two further shipmates were to be travelling to Rome and they were all to be borne by that old faithful barque, The Angel of Northumbria. The now ancient (by current marine standards) ship was certainly showing the signs of its age and had been patched up here and there and it could not travel through the waters as fast as it once had. Nevertheless it was a reliable and comfortable vessel and perfectly adequate for its purpose. It was also to be very lightly laden, which would help it to travel through the seas at a greater rate of knots. So, apart from a few sparse pieces of luggage, the only real item of cargo was to be the box containing two volumes of the Codex and Ceolfrith's change of habit and undergarments. Ceolfrith had so constructed the box that one volume was hidden in a compartment at the bottom of the container. This knowledge was his sole preserve and he chose not to share the existence of this secret area with his shipmates. A second volume was placed above it separated by a false floor. Unless you were aware of this device, and as no other person was privy to the deception, you would not easily tell it had been concealed. The clothing was placed above the visible volume and the wooden box locked with a sturdy padlock. The key to this lock was kept around Ceolfrith's neck providing a base metal companion to the silver cross he had been given on his ordination. The box, which was quite weighty, was carried aboard by the young crew mates and placed carefully in Ceolfrith's cabin on the deck of the ship.

Quite unceremoniously, after a quiet prayer of dedication by the former abbot and crew, the Angel slipped its moorings and glided out of the river Wear and out into the North Sea. No service of commendation by local dignitaries and no group of well wishers waving off our crew, as had happened with Bede's initial journey. The dawn departure was witnessed only by gulls scavenging for food for their hungry offspring. Their ear piecing cawing, cut through the mist shrouding the boat from the sight of sleepy Sunter Land denizens, rising for another day of life's struggle. The gulls ceased their shrill alarm and flew off to feed their offspring and an eerie silence returned. This was punctuated by the call of the captain's commands to an obedient crew which now included the priest. Eschewing his holy orders momentarily for the necessities of helping to propel the ship through the icy waters, he breathed in the fresh sea air and took one final look at the monastery which had been his home for so many years.

Although the crew had made this same journey on numerous occasions with Benet, Bede and Ceolfrith, nothing was taken for granted and the most diligent care was used to navigate a way down the east coast. Land was kept in sight at all times, providing comfort to the sailors yet reminding them of the submerged rocky dangers present all the while. The journey was to be of an express nature with only the minimum of stops. There was to be only one scheduled courtesy visit to Canterbury, in order to present a volume of the Codex to the archbishop for his viewing, approval and blessing for their mission. Then there would be the minimum of stops to replenish food and water. These few diversions would facilitate their earliest arrival at their destination of Ostia and then they would switch to a smaller craft for onward travel to Rome. So Whitby, formerly overseen by the dearly departed Hilda, was sighted and then left behind just as quickly. The crew pushed on as fast as possible to the southern reaches of the country. After two days progress the vast Thames Estuary hove into sight and, after rounding the headland, the mouth of the River Stour was reached. Using the tide, the Angel was skilfully piloted up the waterway to be moored near the centre of the town, with the cathedral of Canterbury in sight from their dock side.

Here it was Ceolfrith's intention to disembark to pay his respects to the Primate of England, the Archbishop of Canterbury - Bertwald. Ceolfrith had met the archbishop on numerous occasions and it was through his encouragement that he had completed the great Codex enterprise. So it was out of respect and deference to the leader of the Christians of England that he wished to make this detour. There was an ulterior and secondary motive for his visit too. For Bertwald and Wilfred had their differences in the past and Ceolfrith had acted as an arbiter in their long standing dispute. Wilfred had at one point been regarded as a rival for the post of archbishop but his rather strident views and abrasive manner had alienated him amongst the country's bishops. Bertwald had won the election and Ceolfrith had been instrumental in reconciling the two. The Bishopric of Hexham was given to Wilfred as a sop but he had never been Bertwald's biggest fan. Ceolfrith was always an advocate for unity within the Church and sought to be a means of healing whenever he could. He hoped to repair some of the damage caused by Wilfred's aggressive behaviour and wished to assure Archbishop Bertwald of his loyal support.

The box was unlocked and the holy volume transferred to a sturdy leather satchel and safely fastened with straps and buckles. Jean delegated the task of carrying the load to a young sailor, Stephen, a strong lithe youth, anxious to please. Tomas and the other young crew member Henry stayed with the boat whilst the trio made their way to the cathedral. It was their task to replenish stocks whilst their shipmates were away on Church business and it was intended that they would set sail early the following day.

Although extremely heavy, Stephen made light work of carrying the satchel and its contents. Jean and Ceolfrith struggled at times to keep up with their young companion but eventually arrived at the archbishop's residence. The party were led to a reception room by the hospitable monk responsible for welcoming guests. Refusing his kind offer of refreshment, he disappeared to refer their appearance to a more senior colleague. Stephen was glad to be able to rest from his exertions and sat alongside Jean. Meanwhile Ceolfrith paced up and down anxiously, prompting Jean to invite him to be seated. After five minutes wait their patience was rewarded when their welcoming monk returned and held open the door, as if to herald the arrival of a more auspicious representative.

Ceolfrith's face visibly betrayed his disappointment at the important personage who presented himself to them. It was not the esteemed Archbishop of Canterbury, his beloved friend Bertwald. It seemed that their request to see the archbishop had either been ignored by the monk who had welcomed them, or his mission had been intercepted by the eminence who now stood before them. That eminence was none other than Canon Kenric, right hand man to Archbishop Bertwald and scourge of those who would dare question his authority. Ostensibly a man with an obsequious demeanour, his way was to try and catch you off guard with flattery and compliments. But anyone who spent any amount of time in his presence knew him to be a dangerous man, a wolf in sheep's clothing and not to be trusted. Ceolfrith was well aware of his fawning subterfuge and was not taken in by him. He had crossed swords with him many times and in truth it was Kenric who Ceolfrith meant when he referred to the dark forces in the Church. He had encountered numerous objections to the work of the Codex from the Canon and many obstacles had been put in Monkwearmouth/Jarrow's way since the work had been commissioned. Kenric bowed to his visitor and an insincere smile traced its way across his face as he greeted them.

"Ah my dear Ceolfrith and our friends from the north! Welcome to our humble abode of Canterbury. It is by the grace of God that you have arrived safely, borne no doubt on those inhospitable waters of the great North Sea. It is a tribute to the Divine Father that you are able to survive at all in those hostile northern lands that even our Roman brothers found so difficult to tame. To what do we owe this great honour?" All the while Kenric's weasel words were accompanied by the wringing of his hands, sweat glistening in the room's gloomy light. Ceolfrith twisted his nose and sighed as he chose the words of his reply carefully.

"Canon Kenric I am sure you are in no doubt as to our purpose here. The message I sent via the brother who greeted us was clear and for the ears of His Holiness our brother in Christ and archbishop of these lands, Bertwald. I would be obliged if you'd make him aware of our arrival as I believe he eagerly awaits it." Ceolfrith knew that Kenric was perfectly aware of his mission in Canterbury and if he was trying to pretend otherwise his eyes betrayed him. For whilst Kenric spoke and, as he listened to Ceolfrith's reply, his gaze was constantly drawn to the leather satchel resting at Stephen's feet.

"I suppose my lord Ceolfrith that it is to do with the endeavours you and your brother monks have been engaged in for so long in the unwelcoming surroundings of that frozen place you regard as home, namely the holy Codex." Kenric's admission was accompanied by his slimy grin, as if he were giving his unadulterated approval. "But you must realise that our leader is engaged in the great work of the Gospel and that there are many projects which demand his attention. I suggest therefore that you leave your great opus in my care and I will ensure that he sees it as soon as possible." He waved his arm as if to emphasis how reasonable his suggestion was. "In fact, I also suggest you surrender the whole enterprise into our care and we will ensure that the volume is transported to our Holy Father in Rome, with all due ceremony that such a magnificent and important representation of the Word of God deserves!"

Ceolfrith stepped up to his adversary so that there was the minimum of space between them and said,

"Kenric! Let us dispense with these tiresome pleasantries. As your superior I demand that you make Bertwald aware that we wish to see him and you do so immediately. Please do not try my patience further."

Kenric made no pretence of amiability and returned Ceolfrith's stare. Deferring to the more senior cleric he nodded to the monk still holding open the door and within a few short minutes the Monkwearmouth party was ushered in to see the archbishop. Bertwald's welcome was as sincere and warm as Kenric's had been false and tepid. The Codex was laid out on a table and the archbishop and his friend pored over the volume with Bertwald audibly gasping at the sight before him. All the while Kenric hovered over their shoulders, grim faced as he tried to glimpse the illuminated text.

"Ceolfrith!" exclaimed Bertwald, "It is a masterpiece, truly inspired by the Holy Spirit of God. You must give my warmest congratulations to Bede and his team of scribes at Jarrow. For they have worked diligently and I warrant for long hours these many years." The archbishop could scarcely contain his delight and broke off his examination of the Codex to embrace Ceolfrith, nodding his head in disbelief at the quality of the work. Kenric moved from foot to foot in irritation, occasionally offering a false smile of approval to his master the archbishop. He didn't bother with this confection of falsehood when Ceolfrith looked his way, knowing that smarmy affectation was lost on him.

Ceolfrith accepted the generous praise of the archbishop and, deflecting the Canon's further interrupted offer to take charge of the transportation to Rome, told Bertwald how he had dedicated the work to the current Pope Gregory the Second. He would not be satisfied until he had personally delivered the volume into the pontiff's hands. However Kenric, with customary faux concern for Ceolfrith and his party, did manage to secure the archbishop's agreement that a marine escort should be provided for the Angel of Northumbria and its crew. This would provide safe cover until the Angel had navigated its way through the English Channel, as French pirate ships had as of late been providing a nuisance to English commercial shipping. Kenric was so effusive in his mock concern that a neutral observer would have been easily deceived into thinking the Canon's fears were genuine. So Ceolfrith reluctantly agreed to this condition and the party made to return to their vessel with the archbishop's blessing. The volume was carefully placed back into its protective satchel and Stephen, who had been an interested and silent observer to the proceedings, now assumed in all seriousness his custodial duties. When they arrived back at the jetty the volume was returned safely to the box on board the Angel and secured by Ceolfrith with the robust lock. He kissed the key and placed it round his neck. Meanwhile the crew prepared for their departure in their usual professional manner.

Early next morning the Angel manoeuvred slowly down the River Stour where it would meet the larger escort vessel at the river's mouth. Sure enough a rendezvous was made with a triple masted ship, which had more in common with naval warship than the smaller boat it was meant to protect. A dozen or so hands could be seen in readiness, as they prepared to let slip the anchor of the ship. When the Angel sailed past it, the name of the escort was picked out in gold lettering and read, Kelcey. Jean used semaphore signalling to his fellow captain to follow at a safe distance, as he was concerned about the potential greater speed and power of the bigger vessel. Jean remarked to his fellow crew that Kelcey meant 'ship victory' and that it must have been used for military purposes in the past. And so the journey to Rome began in earnest (save for a replenishment stop at Cadiz) and the two vessels proceeded line astern out of the harbour and into the English Channel.

Steady progress was made through the Channel with the Kelcey shadowing the Angel as the day grew shorter and darkness encroached. The two boats had successfully made it to the end of the English Channel and had rounded the Brest peninsula when Jean had expected the Kelcey to relinquish its duties and return to Canterbury. Instead he became slightly perturbed by the larger vessel drawing closer to his boat on the starboard side. The French coast was still clearly visible on the port side as the Kelcey came alongside the Angel. Jean could observe that the reason for the unexpected turn of speed was due to the application of twelve oarsmen, six to each side of the Kelcey. Suddenly and without warning the escort ship veered to the left and made for the Angel. The older boat was less manoeuvrable and slower than its potential adversary and Jean and his incredulous crew could only watch helplessly as they were struck a glancing blow midships. The Kelcey then turned about and prepared for another strike. Jean could only look on forlornly as the Kelcey picked up speed for a full on collision with his boat. The creaking and cracked woods of the Angel had withstood the first blow but succumbed to the more direct second. The ageing timbers snapped under the pressure of their false friend and water gushed into the hold and the boat immediately began to list. The severity of the collision had catapulted the two young deck hands Henry and Stephen, into the cold sea and they could be seen bobbing for their lives.

Jean gave the command to abandon ship and a small row boat (used usually for ship to shore transportation) was lowered by Tomas who, seeing that the lads had been cast unceremoniously overboard, was anxious to use the craft to rescue them. He threw a rope ladder down the sagging side of the boat and urged Ceolfrith to climb down. Somehow he had managed to drag the box containing the Codex from his cabin on deck to the edge of the boat. Tomas told him to climb down and he would lower the box. Deftly he dangled the box one handedly over the side, the blood vessels on his arm bulging with the strain and Ceolfrith drew on all his strength to grasp it. Tomas quickly scrambled down before the effort became too much for the monk and placed the box in the stern of the row boat. Jean leapt from the deck and into the sea and disappeared from sight into the murky depths. Almost immediately, to the relief of his two friends, he rose to the surface and clambered into the boat. Not an accomplished swimmer, Jean lay in the bow gasping for air. Whilst he recovered his breath Tomas shouted,

"Quickly! Ceolfrith take an oar and let's get away before the Angel sinks and drags us down with it. Then we must see if we can find the lads." The former abbot duly obeyed and put his back into a synchronised stroke with his rowing mate and before too long they had travelled a hundred yards between themselves and the Angel. They stopped and recovered their breath and watched helplessly as their former floating home slowly slunk below the level of the sea, with only white bubbling spume as evidence of its existence. Unable to permit themselves the luxury of self pity, they frantically rowed in a circular motion looking for the two hands.

The Kelcey meanwhile had stolen away unnoticed in order to make its way back to its home port, having accomplished its objective of sinking the ship it was meant to escort. Sinister deep male voices could be heard cheering and singing as the captain declared a grog reward for their successful efforts. Sails were hoisted to facilitate its progress and the oarsmen were permitted to raise their blades, leaving the propulsion of the ship to the elements.

After several hours of fruitless searching and being pulled further down the coast, the crew of the row boat reluctantly gave up hope of finding the lads alive and made for the strand. Exhausted, they beached the boat on the shores of France as dawn rose over the bent grass clad dunes. After the three men hopped out of the boat, Tomas and Jean dragged it up the beach so that the English Channel could not claim it back. The trio collapsed on to their sandy bed, wheezing and coughing all the while trying to recover some sort of composure. The only evidence of their voyage, the box containing the Codex, sat in silent accusation on board their means of escape.

Chapter Nine
Hwaetberht

It is now over three weeks since Ceolfrith set off for Rome, leaving his letter of resignation for Hwaetberht to open five days after he left. A personal missive for the eyes of the Prior only, it summarised Ceolfrith's wishes. He had also left a second letter sealed and only to be opened and read when the monks were in convocation. I returned to Jarrow after receiving the news of the convocation from Wilfred. I rode back to the monastery on the horse given me by Newton, after picking up my mother from Heddon. We returned the donkey to Jacob at Felling and my mother completed the final part of the journey on my horse. I had to endure an endless interrogation from her about the purpose of the convocation called by Father Prior and I genuinely wished that Ceolfrith had not taken me into his confidence, so that I could answer her questions more honestly. I hope equivocating does not count as lying, otherwise I will be doing penance for some considerable time.

Since returning from Hexham, and after ensuring that the monastery at Jarrow was safe in the care of a few postulants and lay workers, I had been resident at Monkwearmouth for nearly a week. The convocation had been further delayed due to the difficulty in our community reassembling. Monks had to return from Lindisfarne, Whitby and York as well as two from Scotland. Adverse weather and difficulty in communicating had led to the delay. Now it had been rescheduled for tomorrow with the last of the community due to return this evening.

I took the opportunity of a lull in proceedings to have a quiet meeting with Hwaetberht in order to confess that Ceolfrith had confided his actions to me, though I was unaware of the finer points. It was testament to the magnanimity of the man that he took the news in his stride and was not offended that the Ceolfrith had chosen a relative junior as his confidante. He had guessed that the contents contained information of such importance but humility had prevented him from such a far reaching assumption before reading it himself. I assured the prospective abbot of my full support and we left on good terms. The monastic day concluded as usual with the service of Compline, which was the first time a full compliment of monks had been in attendance in years. An atmosphere of excited anticipation was all pervading and I found sleep difficult to come by. But I knew that it would not be long before the cycle of our day would begin again.

The meeting was scheduled to commence after a con-celebrated Eucharist with Hwaetberht as the main celebrant. After the ceremony we all processed into the refectory which had been cleared and the tables moved so that all participants had sight of one another. Following a prayer of dedication, Hwaetberht rose to his feet and addressed us,

"My dear confrères in Christ Jesus I stand before you today at the request of our beloved Abbot Ceolfrith. Before he left for Rome he gave me a sealed letter which was to be read only to the full assembled brothers." He flourished the letter contained within a large envelope with the unmistakable red seal of the former abbot. Ensuring that everyone could see, he carefully broke the seal and withdrew the letter. Hwaetberht was a short rotund man, the very physical antithesis of Ceolfrith. Nevertheless he had his own innate aura of authority different to, yet similar to the author of the letter. Clearing his throat and drawing himself up to his full height he began to read,

"Dear brothers in Christ and fellow colleagues of Monkwearmouth and Jarrow I pray that the Spirit of the Living God and the love of the Father and the peace of Our Lord Jesus be with you this day.

By the time you hear these words I trust that, by the grace of God, I will be in the presence of our Holy father the Pope and he will be blessed by the work of our hands, namely the holy Codex. Truly I feel that this is the consummation of my work. I have, I think, devoted too much time to this enterprise, perhaps to the detriment of the well being of our community.

To this end therefore, it is with a sense of achievement but with a heavy heart that I must tender my resignation as your Abbot Father. I have been privileged to serve our community since the death of Abbot Benet. But I

feel that I am not the man to continue to lead our community. I lack the energy to carry this great responsibility. I ask you, in all humility, to grant this request with immediate effect.

I have one further request to make of you and that is that my successor should be your current Father Prior - Hwaetberht. He has both the experience and the holiness to lead Monkwearmouth Jarrow into the future. I refer you to Holy Scriptures when considering your decision, In the Letter to the Hebrews chapter thirteen verse seven it says, 'Remember your leaders, who spoke the word of God to you. Consider the outcome of their way of life and imitate their faith.' And then again in the same chapter, verse seventeen, 'Have confidence in your leaders and submit to their authority, because they keep watch over you as those who must give an account. Do this so that their work will be a joy, not a burden, for that would be of no benefit to you. I hope that the Word of God, which is alive and active, and inspired by the Holy Spirit guides you during this process.'

So my dear confrères, God willing, I will return to you as a brother, only a monk. A mere man of God! The position I so earnestly desired when I first joined our monastery. So I will be restored to my first love. It will please me to end my days as I began, as a servant to the servants of Christ.

Yours, a humble servant of Christ
Ceolfrith"

Hwaetberht folded the letter and returned it to its envelope. Although he had been appraised, by Bede, of its probable contents, it nevertheless visibly moved him to tears. Using the index finger of his right hand to dry his cheek he sniffed to prevent any further show of emotion and began.

"My friends I am shocked and surprised, as you must be, by Ceolfrith's words but it is clear that he has given much thought to this course of action and his mind is set. I am sure that he did not come to this decision lightly and that much prayer and spiritual consideration has been expended. However, I am not one to impose his request upon the community without discussion and the opportunity for you to give vent to your feelings. I therefore throw the meeting open, so that I may hear your thoughts. I request that you do so in all respect and in cognisance of our former abbot's wishes." With that, as if exhausted by the news, Hwaetberht almost slumped into his seat and awaited their opinions.

There then followed a long discussion where arguments and counter arguments were put for and against the appointment of Hwaetberht as abbot. The unifying effects of Chad and Ced at Hexham had not fully worked through the returning Hexham contingent and they took the opportunity to air long felt grievances. However delegates who had been working away from the community, and had a degree of objectivity, were able to give a good account of Hwaetberht's tenure as prior. This was reinforced by many of the resident monks. A clear majority though did emerge for the appointment of Hwaetberht but the objectors still represented a vocal and articulate minority and were proving to be an obstinate obstacle to his accession. It seemed, as the meeting was drifting to an impasse, that this was an opportune time for me to make my contribution. There was a natural break in the proceedings and we adjourned for refreshments and a comfort stop. Those brothers less confident in public speaking began to canvass me informally for my opinion. They listened attentively to my thoughts and then urged me to speak more formally within the context of the convocation. I was sufficiently buoyed up by the support of my colleagues that I determined to speak at the first opportunity. As we reconvened I caught Hwaetberht's eye and he indicated that the floor was mine.

"Thank you friends for your kind attention and I would urge you, with all unanimity, to give your blessing to Father Hwaetberht in his desire to serve our community. With his customary humility I think our current prior and potential abbot has not professed sufficiently the unique service he has already given. Whilst Ceolfrith was preoccupied with the production of the Codex, and this activity consumed vast amounts of his time and energy, he was reassured with the knowledge that the smooth running of our vast monastery and its interests were in safe and capable hands. I have personally witnessed the tireless work Father Prior has done within our community and the surrounding environs. Many lay people here and at Jarrow depend upon the professional administration he has demonstrated. Their livelihoods are intertwined with the prosperity of our two houses.

His attention to detail is without compare and whenever he has had to administer discipline it has been done with love and consideration. I have often been the subject of his gentle reproofs and I can vouch as to his excellent and practical advice.

These are the qualities which our esteemed Abbot Ceolfrith has been so admiring of and which has persuaded him to recommend Hwaetberht as his successor. I truly believe, if there were a more suitable and qualified candidate, then Ceolfrith would have been the first to recognise him. The fact that he could only bring himself to resign 'in absentia' shows that he wishes you to make this decision free from any pressure or authority he could exert. Sometimes we fail to notice the qualities of those so close to us and I urge you to reflect prayerfully and objectively on the words of our previous Abbot Ceolfrith.

In summation if I can paraphrase the words of St. Luke in the Acts of the Apostles when talking about Gamaliel. If Ceolfrith's recommendation is of human origin then Hwaetberht's abbatialship will fail but if it is from God then we will be going against His wishes and we will find ourselves in the unenviable position of fighting God. I am sure you will agree that this is the worst of all possible positions."

I held as many of my brother monks in my gaze as I could, as I scanned the room before sitting. By now we had been meeting for most of the day, punctuated only by our divine office and refreshment breaks. No work of a physical or intellectual nature was being done today. Hwaetberht excused himself from proceedings allowing a further hour for discussion and to come to our decision. Old ground was revisited but in a more positive way and a consensus was arrived at not by means of a vote but by dealing with outstanding objections. There being no remaining barriers to Hwaetberht's accession then the most junior monk was deputed to relay our decision to him and request his attendance at out meeting.

Hwaetberht bowed in acceptance of the community's unanimous decision and spontaneous applause broke out. He raised his arm in a vain attempt to curtail the clapping and the more boisterous monks began to bang the tables. Suddenly our unalloyed joy was rudely interrupted by the grinding of the large wooden door bursting open and there stood a dishevelled Jean with his companion Tomas. The assembly turned as one and held their collective breath as the captain approached our newly 'crowned' abbot. He knelt in respectful abeyance and as he rose to his feet he exclaimed,

"Father Prior I regret to inform you that your dear friend Abbot Ceolfrith ..... is dead!"

Chapter Ten
A Death In France

The three survivors washed up at St. Nazaire, a little fishing village in France. Fishing nets and boats littered the shore and swarthy bearded men watched as they hauled their small row boat up the shingle. In more sanguine times the village would have proved a welcome place for the visitor to alight and converse amiably with the local residents. But the trio had just escaped a watery grave and were in no mood to take in the niceties of the tourist. With the aid of native French speaking Jean, they were able engage with the fishermen and barter their boat (using some gold Ceolfrith had brought for emergency purposes) for a cart pulled by an aged horse. A grumpy French man, of a similar vintage to the horse, took ownership of the craft and gold and grunted some sort of thanksgiving. It was obvious to even the most naïve observer that he had been the beneficiary of the deal but his shrugged body language would make you think that he had just been robbed.

The three men determined to travel overland through central France and then across the Alps to northern Italy and on to Rome. Here they would deliver their sacred load and the recent tragic events served only to increase their resolve to secure justice for their two dead shipmates. The journey would be longer and even more hazardous than the one they had originally planned. However it was now in the knowledge that their very existence on earth was threatened by the dark forces Ceolfrith had always feared. Those dark forces found their embodiment in Kenric and his mercenary men who had executed his fiendish plan. A plan he would no doubt soon discover had not proved entirely successful. What Ceolfrith had long suspected had manifested itself in the most cruel attack which had claimed the lives of two innocent young men. The two young men had not been personally known to Ceolfrith before leaving Monkwearmouth and sea salt was rubbed into the wound of grief by the knowledge that this was their first voyage. Survival is a powerful motivating force and, now that their immediate danger had passed, Ceolfrith turned his thoughts to the missing boys.

"It is not beyond the power of God that Henry and Stephen have survived just as we did." he told his two companions. His faith had always been a shining example to all who knew Ceolfrith but Tomas averted his gaze and Jean coughed and spluttered out the remnants of sea water from his lungs. They both nodded a tepid agreement but felt that even their long time friend's faith was being severely tested. "Let us kneel in prayer and commit their destiny to the living and Almighty God, who set the sea its boundaries and threw the stars into the night sky. For it is He who dictates when we are born and when we die. If, in His mercy, He sees fit to rescue our friends then we will rejoice but if God has welcomed them into His bosom then our rejoicing will be the greater." The three men knelt in humble adoration and in remembrance of the powerful sea which had almost claimed their lives and prayed for their colleagues' souls. Ceolfrith concluded their time of reflection with the Lord's Prayer and they all struggled to their feet. Tomas stroked the horse that was to bear them on the next part of their journey. As he held the reins Jean lifted the box containing the volumes and secured it to the rear of the cart. He helped Ceolfrith up and then followed his lead, finally thrusting an arm out to pull Tomas on to the vehicle. Tomas then reclaimed the reins and steered them all away from their temporary haven.

They had to act quickly and in the utmost secrecy as news of their survival would surely get back to Kenric and he would not rest until he had possession of the Codex and had eliminated its custodians. Unseen to Ceolfrith and what remained of his crew (who had more pressing worries to contend with) the Kelcey, on seeing the three men escape from their sinking boat and struggle vainly to save their friends, had deployed its own lifeboat and two agents of the dastardly Canon Kenric had been landed on the French shore. It was their express purpose to 'deal' with the crew of the stricken Angel and recover its cargo, if it had survived the impact.

Kenric's men had landed thirty or so miles away and, after signalling to their mother boat, began to make their way inland. They had the benefit of maps, documents and more gold than Ceolfrith had, in order to help ease their investigations and pursuit of the Monkwearmouth contingent. They were two of Kenric's most accomplished agents and had enjoyed generous financial rewards for their efforts in the past. They had departed from the safety of the Kelcey in the knowledge that the recovery or destruction of the Codex would be similarly rewarded. Both groups had the same initial destination in mind, namely Nantes, being the nearest city on the major route to the Alps and on through the pass to Italy.

Meanwhile the Kelcey had made its unerring way back to Canterbury and its captain had reported back to Kenric. Ostensibly a man of God (though perhaps which god is not known) Kenric had long coveted the work done by the Northumbrian monks. He had visited Monkwearmouth and had spent time with Ceolfrith at Jarrow and overseen some of the work of the scribes. Ceolfrith had never taken to him and thought him a shallow superficial person. This had not gone unnoticed by Kenric who made a mental note and filed it under, adversary to be taken down a peg or two, in his encyclopaedic memory. Bede had escaped Kenric's machinations, having been away on monastery business, so the two had never met. Kenric thought Northumbria a wild and hostile area and regarded those Tynesiders an unteachable lot. His attempts to recruit agents to his cause from the area had proved difficult, though no one was sure if he had been unsuccessful. It was thought that the disloyal group which had attached themselves to Hexham may have provided fertile ground for his wiles.

He also had designs on the Archbishopric of Canterbury and had often undermined his superior. He was careful enough not to openly betray his true colours in public but he was always a destabilising force in the background. In fact he had supported Wilfred in his attempt to become Archbishop of Canterbury but after this had failed he had managed to ingratiate himself into Bertwald's service. Favours had been called in and palms greased and, much to the chagrin of the archbishop, he found one of his main rivals as his right hand man.

Kenric had developed a network of spies and informants and had his finger on the pulse of every abbey and monastery in the land. Well nearly every one, as Monkwearmouth and Jarrow had evaded his oversight, though he knew second hand of the progress of Bede's work. He had determined to take control of the Codex and so thereby denigrate the role of Jarrow and

Monkwearmouth in the Church's eyes. He would then pass the work off as his own initiative and increase his standing with Rome. So it was important that his delegates retrieve the Codex, if it had survived the impact. As far as he knew there was only one volume in existence and the Kelcey captain's report, on the ship's return to Canterbury, seemed to suggest that this and Ceolfrith had survived the sinking of the Angel. He was informed of the two trusted henchmen who were now in hot pursuit and this was sufficient to satisfy his master's concerns. Kenric dismissed the captain with instructions to keep him informed of progress and made off to report his version of events to Archbishop Bertwald. He straightened his habit ensuring that the folds fell from his waist and opened the door to his superior's office; a custom which irked Bertwald who would have preferred the formality of a respectful knock. As he entered the room he could see that the archbishop was entertaining a guest. Glasses with the remnants of ruby red wine sat on the desk and a monk glad in the Benedictine garb sat opposite the archbishop.

"Forgive me my Lord Archbishop I did not realise that you were engaged but I am sure that you would not mind the interruption." Bertwald had grown accustomed to Kenric's presumption but his haughty behaviour still rather rankled. "I am afraid I have some extremely sad news of huge import." This prompted a more attentive attitude from his two listeners and seeing he had their undivided attention he continued. "I am so grieved to tell you my Lord, that the Angel of Northumbria has been sunk at sea and all aboard have been lost! The captain of the Kelcey tells me that, despite their valiant attempts to save the crew, their efforts were in vain and they are devastated at the loss of their fellow seafarers." Kenric's expression of remorse at the exaggerated loss of life was truly convincing and he could even be seen to wipe away a tear from his eyes. Of course he neglected to mention his agents' part in the debacle and how two of them were now hunting down the survivors. He was well versed in being 'economical with the truth' (this was a basic requirement of his dark arts) but he had no compunction in outright lying to achieve his ends.

Kenric explained how it seemed the Angel had sailed too close to the French shore and was holed by unseen rocks. He said that the Kelcey, being the bigger ship, could not easily manoeuvre to its aid and so had been hampered by the dangerous rocks and the inclement weather. His story was so well embellished with detail that you would have thought that he had been an onboard eye witness instead of a downright liar. Bertwald listened attentively without interruption and seeing that Kenric had finished he answered,

"Indeed Kenric the news you bear is the worst possible and we are deeply saddened by the loss of our dear friends. We must act with the utmost speed to do what we can for our brothers. It is too late in this life, and I am sure they will be with the Father, but we must afford them full respect in death and give them a Christian burial. Their bodies will have washed up on the shore and have been recovered by the local people. Your captain will be able to locate where their vessel went down and you, through careful investigation, can retrieve our dear friends' bodies and give them all the rights in death our great faith offers."

Kenric took a sharp intake of breath and never thought that he would be delegated to take charge of so menial and distasteful a task. He stuttered a form of words in protest but Bertwald would brook no objection and took this opportunity to introduce his, so far, silent but interested guest.

"Kenric may I introduce to you Abbot Gregory from Lindisfarne who has monastic business in mother Rome and is paying us a respectful visit on his way. I am sure he will accompany you on your quest." Gregory nodded his silent assent and Bertwald continued, "How quickly can you muster your ship to this purpose? Gregory has made the long journey from Lindisfarne by land, so would be glad to sail with you part way and help you give those last rites to our faithful friends." Kenric, inwardly panicking yet outwardly serene, tried to think quickly how long he could stall the archbishop and his new helpmate. He needed time for his two agents, already in France, to accomplish their objective before he began his pointless quest. He resorted to his tried and tested tactic of flattery. His encyclopaedic brain clicked into action and he recalled what his network of informants had reported about this cleric from the far north. He remembered that a monk there had a reputation for expounding scientific theories and had been elected Abbot of Lindisfarne Monastery. This had proved rather controversial, as some felt these theories ran counter to the spread of the Gospel and might negate the existence of God.

"Ah Father Gregory! Although I have not had the honour of meeting you I have heard much about you and your interest in the power of science. I know that you are well versed in these new ways. Some say your views undermine our faith and will kill all belief in God. I am sure that this a view shared by short sighted brothers who do not have the benefit of your vast learning and great knowledge. I would deem it a blessing if you were to share this knowledge with us as I feel Canterbury should be a leading depository of scientific learning"

Instinctively Kenric's body language became fawning and submissive and he rubbed his hands in obsequiousness. He oozed insincerity! Nevertheless he had activated Gregory's interest in a subject he loved to hold forth on.

"Canon Kenric I assure you that science does not and will never displace the Eternal God. No! In fact it is a testament to His greatness and attests to His wonder. The God who made the stars and set them in place also made the tiny worlds within the sands on our shore" Gregory realised that he could quite easily talk for hours on this subject but also understood that there were other pressing topics so thought a more simple illustration was required. Looking around the room he picked up one of the wine glasses and pressed the glass with his fingers and held it up to the light. The impression of four finger prints could be seen clearly against the background light. "See this goblet brother and see the imprint of my fingers upon it?" In the cold air the marks of his fingers would be seen only momentarily before they would as quickly disappear. "Did you see those whirls made by my fingers on the glass? Well I have studied, over the years, those impressions made by many people and, you know Kenric, I have yet to see any two alike. We all have our own individual designs upon our fingers and I think this is reflective of how our bodies are constructed. I believe in years to come more expert scientists than I will be able to prove how unique we all are. See my Lord Kenric, science shows how great our God is and how he cares for each one of us. There is nothing to fear from science. It can only increase the wonder and beauty of God's magnificent creation."

Kenric was most adroit at finding his opponents weak points (as he saw them) and exploiting them for his own ends. He had succeeded in diverting attention from Bertwald's question and bought himself enough time to answer his senior's original question.

"Most interesting Abbot Gregory and I look forward to continuing our discussions on our voyage of mercy. I am afraid good Archbishop Bertwald that this can not take place for at least four days yet. The Kelcey suffered a little damage in its heroic attempts at rescue and will need this time for repair." This at least was true but he failed to mention that the damage had been self inflicted in the ruthless assault on the Angel. Bertwald accepted Kenric's explanation and arrangements were made with Gregory to join the ship. Kenric then left their company to plot his next step.

*   *   *   *   *   *

Ceolfrith and his two friends arrived in Nantes, a busy town, and they sought shelter for the night at an inn. Jean man-handled the box containing the Codex up to Ceolfrith's room and Tomas saw to the stabling and feeding of the animal and joined the other two for a meal before retiring for the night. Next morning, prior to leaving for the city of Tours, Ceolfrith found a local cartographer who was able to sell him a map for the rest of their journey. On it, the map maker plotted a number of monasteries and abbeys where they could seek refuge and sustenance along the way.

So began the journey in earnest across France and to the foothills of the Alps where they would hire a guide to negotiate the mountain passes to Italy. Their progress was patchy as it was hampered by torrential rain and strong winds for two days. Their animal struggled against the elements and most of the time the party of travellers walked alongside the cart guiding the beleaguered animal. Eventually the mountains were in sight as they grew nearer the border. Ceolfrith caught a heavy cold and, as he was struggling more than the horse against the lashing rain, they decided to break early for the night at the lively market town of Langres near to Tours. They were fortunate to get rooms at an hostelry in the centre of the bustling town. Jean unpacked the box with the Codex to Ceolfrith's room and he and Tomas took the horse and cart to the stables on the outskirts of town. Ceolfrith made his way from his bedroom to the communal room downstairs frequented by male farm workers and labourers. He ordered three meals and secured a table for the return of his friends and sat down with his drinks. His hacking cough drew fleeting attention from the garrulous farmers quaffing ale and discussing their workday woes. Out of the knot of men a tall figure approached Ceolfrith's table. From his appearance and dress he was obviously not of farming stock and, as he raised his voice to be heard over the hubbub of the men of the earth, an unmistakeable English accent could be detected.

"Sir, I see you are cursed with that awful cough. I am, my friend, an apothecary from England, on research business here in France and if you would permit me I think this draught may help you." He took a small glass phial from beneath his cloak and slipped the contents into Ceolfrith's drink. He lifted the glass and offered it to Ceolfrith who at first declined his overtures. However on further reassurance from the plausible stranger that the draught would produce an immediate benefit, Ceolfrith drank it. Almost at once he had a feeling of total well being and thanked the stranger for his assistance. Then there followed a strange ebbing and flowing as if he were on board the Angel again, bobbing up and down on the ocean. He stood and held on to the arm of the stranger who motioned to another man for help. "Let us get you to your room brother, I am sure you will feel better away from all this noise." The second man took his other arm and they managed to get him up a steep flight of stairs to his room, warmed by an open fire crackling in the corner. There they lay him upon his bed and stood menacingly over him, fixing their gaze on the pupils of his eyes, which were becoming ever more dilated. Ceolfrith struggled to focus and their features grew large then small before his eyes.

"The box sir," said the first stranger politely yet with firm menace. Ceolfrith clutched the key round his neck defying him to claim it and the man nodded to his accomplice. "Just break it open and get the book."

Taking out his sword, his assistant obeyed the order and forced open the box, threw the few items of clothing across the room and held up the Codex victoriously.

"My master Kenric sends his regards and thanks you for all your assistance," said the bogus apothecary, whilst his accomplice had opened the Codex and tore the frontispiece from the volume, scrunched it up and tossed it into the fire. He was about to repeat the process when he was prevented from doing so by his master.

"What in the name of God's blood do you think you are doing? Have you taken leave of your senses? Kenric wants the volume intact you idiot." He took the book off him and placed it carefully in a bag he had brought for the purpose. "Now good Ceolfrith we will leave you as we see that you still feel unwell. Hopefully the draught I gave you will do its work"

The two men stole out of the inn with the Codex and made their way from the town. Ceolfrith struggled to regain control of his body and forced himself up from his bed and then quickly collapsed to the floor retching and vomiting. He sank into a deep sleep.

Jean and Tomas returned to be informed by the innkeeper that Ceolfrith had been taken to his room, as he was unwell, by two of his 'friends.' Sensing something amiss the two men ascended the stairs to find Ceolfrith comatose on the floor. They gently lifted him on to the bed and spent the rest of the night tending to his fever, in turns dowsing him with water in a vain attempt to reduce his temperature. As dawn broke Ceolfrith regained consciousness and thought he was well enough to recommence his journey. However it was clear he was too ill and his friends took him to the Church of the Blessed Twin Martyrs in Langres. Here he summoned all his strength to instruct his two friends. They were to be his final instructions. He asked for parchment, ink and a quill which the parish priest was able to supply. Propped up in a makeshift bier in the nave of the church, he scratched a missive for fifteen minutes and, when complete, asked Jean to make sure it was secured in an envelope and then sealed. The letter was returned to him duly sealed with some candle wax and he tentatively wrote the name, Bede, across the envelope.

"Jean, Tomas, I thank you your friendship these many years and I ask your forgiveness for risking your lives on this venture. You have both been faithful servants of Christ and his monastery at Monkwearmouth. But the fate of those two boys hangs heavy upon my heart. Please give my condolences to Henry and Stephen's families and I ask for their forgiveness too. See that Bede gets this letter and implore him to act upon its contents urgently. The fate of years of work now rest in his hands. Like Moses I am destined never to see the Promised Land and Bede must be my Joshua." The two men unconvincingly urged him to seek life over death, to draw on the faith which had seen many people healed over the years at his intercession. But it was obvious to them that their friend was dying. "One final request. Wherever you lay me to rest I ask in the name of Christ Jesus to place the box at my feet. It is most important that box does not fall into Kenric's possession. It must provide silent company for my remains" Jean agreed to his friend's last wish and bowed his head in despair. Ceolfrith raised his head one final time and said,

"Lord into your hands I commend my spirit."

He closed his eyes and died.

Chapter Eleven
Monkwearmouth and Gertrude at Primrose

The whole convocation sat in silence as Jean and Tomas informed us about the events in France. We all gasped as we heard how Henry and Stephen had been so cruelly lost at sea, as a result of the wicked instructions of Kenric. A murmur of disbelief relayed around the vast room at the thought of an alleged godly man, resorting to such devious tactics. Heads were shaken and misericords banged, as some of the more youthful monks stood to express their disgust and desire for retribution. Hwaetberht raised his hand in an authoritative command for order and silence and it was almost instantly obeyed. Tears were then shed as they told us about Ceolfrith's final moments and Hwaetberht, seeing that it was all too much for both the two men reporting the events and their listeners, brought an end to the proceedings. The pair were unkempt and tired and so he ordered that they be fed and watered and given some rest. He would resume further discussions with them later, in the more private and comfortable surroundings of his study. With sighs of resignation they both gratefully accepted this offer and surrendered themselves to the care of two ministering angels, clad in Benedictine black habits.

After Jean and Tomas had been taken from our presence, Hwaetberht led us in prayer for our former Abbot Ceolfrith and the two lost souls of Henry and Stephen. The previous discussions about the niceties of Hwaetberht's succession seemed to have been forgotten by the assembly and there was now a tacit assent to his assuming the role of our leader. Events had overtaken us and we now needed a unity of purpose, we needed a man who could lead us into an uncertain future. The prayer time concluded and, as we monks processed from the meeting, most embraced Abbot Hwaetberht in a sign of support. I retired to my cell and fell on my knees in a time of personal prayer. Once again the Psalms came to my aid:

I lift up my eyes to the mountains - where does my help come from?

My help comes from the Lord - the Maker of heaven and earth.

He will not let your foot slip, he who watches over you will not slumber;
indeed, he who watches over Israel will neither slumber nor sleep.

The Lord watches over you -the Lord is your shade at your right hand;
the sun will not harm you by day - nor the moon by night.

The Lord will keep you from all harm - he will watch over your life;
the Lord will watch over your coming and going,

both now and forever-more.

I am unable to tell you how long I was lost in prayer but I remember being torn from my deep communion with our Creator, in the Holy of Holies, by a knock on my door. That sanctuary where we are allowed to approach the Almighty in the confidence that we will always be heard. That holy audience has been purchased for us through the blood of Our Saviour Jesus Christ. I was informed that Abbot Hwaetberht requested my attendance. The title abbot was used without coercion and quite matter of factly by the junior monk deputed to summons me.

It was I who completed the party of four persons in Abbot Hwaetberht's (as I must learn to call him) study. Jean and Tomas had also been summonsed and had arrived some minutes before me. As we all sat down I recalled that the last time I was in this room was the day I had seen Ceolfrith poring over my great opus. I remembered how strange his behaviour was; animated and excited yet with a sense of foreboding and foreknowledge of the dangers that lay before him.

I dismissed these memories, as I needed all my powers of concentration on the details my two friends were now outlining. This time Tomas took the lead and recounted the whole story again, with Jean adding words of confirmation or something he omitted. They had laid Ceolfrith to rest in the crypt of the Church of the Twin Martyrs at Langres and confirmed he had been afforded all the dignity and final commendations of the Church, by the local bishop, as befits a man of God. Almost as an after thought they also confirmed that the box, which had contained the Codex, was also resting with his body in the crypt. It seemed almost irrelevant, as we tried to assimilate the loss of our great friend, that they also confirmed the Codex was missing, the lock having been forced. They thought that the two mysterious 'friends', the innkeeper had told them about, were responsible. Tomas assumed that these men were agents of Kenric. Ceolfrith had been too delirious to recount any of the evening's events and had been only concerned with writing a letter before he died. As if on cue, Jean pulled out the letter from his tunic and gave it to me. I held the document in front of me with my name inscribed upon it in the unmistakable hand of dear Ceolfrith.

The two men had held us transfixed, as their story unfolded and they now drew to their conclusion as they told us how they had made their way back home as quickly as possible, conscious of the dangers Kenric's henchmen still represented. They had travelled to the Brest Peninsula and found passage up the west coast of England to Cumbria where they had disembarked and trekked overland to Monkwearmouth. They had been surprised to find this route far quicker than their usual way and had saved as much as five days on their return journey. Their story concluded, the two men asked to be excused as they desired to see their families. With heartfelt thanks and further commiserations they departed. After moments of reflection the new abbot said,

"Well Bede, what a harrowing story of murder and betrayal. How despicable that Kenric's men should take advantage of our brother's illness to steal the Codex. Have they no scruples? Have they lost all sight of God? I suppose if you hold the life of two innocent young men so cheap then you will have no qualms about theft. Even if that theft involves stealing the Word of God!"

I could only stand open mouthed, holding Ceolfrith's letter, rendered incapable of action. I caressed the inscription of my name on the envelope knowing that this would have been the last word my dear friend would have written. His state of health at the time of writing was evidenced by the erratic nature of his hand upon the paper. Hwaetberht drew my attention to the letter and suggested I read it in private. I declined this offer saying that I had full trust in him and that I would like him to hear Ceolfrith's final instruction. As we both sat, I carefully unfolded the letter from the envelope and began to read aloud,

"Bede, my dear brother in Christ Jesus,

If you are reading this letter, my friend, then I have gone the way of all flesh and I am resting in the arms of Our Dear Lord. I have fought the good fight and run the race to the end. By now you will also be aware of the events which have preceded my death. The loss of Henry and Stephen lie heavily upon my heart and I ask the Lord to forgive me for not protecting them. I am confident that the Lord will be a safe harbour for the three of us. To Him be all honour glory and praise. My faithful friends Jean and Tomas have acquitted themselves with all honour and bravery and deserve the support of our monastery, as do their families and those of Henry and Stephen. I charge you as part of my last will and testament that this be attended to with all speed.

Forgive me if I ramble on but the fever attacks me with a vengeance. Jean will have told you that those uncaring agents of Kenric have taken our work – the holy Codex. However fear not my dear Bede, for it was not the Codex which they stole but your volume of error filled pages which I asked you to assemble for me. I have a true volume safely with me but I dare not put on paper where this is. I am sure you, and Kenric for that matter, will be able to discover it. I charge you Bede to come and find the volume and transport it safely to its destination. Bring also the second volume as a back up, should that cursed Kenric discover my volume. For he will do everything to prevent its delivery. Again I can not tell you where I secreted it at Monkwearmouth, should this letter fall into the wrong hands. But Bede, look for the tree in the woods and you will find it.

Finally Bede. You are unknown to Kenric and to his men. So I suggest you travel incognito and not in your monastic garb. This will ensure your safety and enable you to travel in relative obscurity. If possible do not travel alone as there is strength in numbers.

So, farewell my friend. Pass on my blessings to Hwaetberht and may he lead our community in all humility and by the grace of God alone. Yours in the name of Our Lord and Saviour Jesus Christ

Ceolfrith"

A tear ran down my cheek as I folded the letter. Hwaetberht sat holding his chin with his left hand, taking in every syllable of his erstwhile friend's words. A thought played itself across my mind. Ceolfrith had referred to two volumes of the Codex and the erroneous volume but had made no mention of the third volume, which I have secreted at Jarrow. A dilemma presented itself to me. I was Hwaetberht's most loyal monk and I had the urge to tell him about my secret volume's location but I was also conscious of Ceolfrith's exhortation to tell no one its whereabouts. In an instant I determined that, in this respect, my loyalty lies with the latter deceased man rather than the former live one. However I am an honest monk and should Hwaetberht ask me directly about the secret volume then I will have no option but to tell him. He was though thinking about a secret volume but not the one at Jarrow but the one Ceolfrith referred to in his letter. The one he had hidden here in Monkwearmouth.

"Ehmm.....Look for the tree in the wood....Of course Bede! Where would you hide a book?" said Hwaetberht. I gulped in disbelief trying not to betray my guilt. Before I could reply he continued, "Within other books!"

He clasped his hand in victory and swept out of the room towards the library. I followed in his wake. It took about five minutes of fruitless pulling out and pushing back volumes before, amongst the defunct, dusty and once erudite books, there it was. Ceolfrith had said he was going to file the imperfect volume here and so had reversed the information he gave me at our last meeting. Hwaetberht carefully withdrew the book and placed it on the table and examined it. Sure enough it was the second perfect volume. Ceolfrith switched the two volumes and suspected that there would be a threat, though at the time he did not know where from.

"We have our missing volume and the other one must be with Ceolfrith's body. In the box I'll warrant. He must have hidden it in a secret compartment and kept its existence from Jean and Tomas. The thieves obviously would not be able to distinguish between them and must have been satisfied with their imperfect haul." Hwaetberht's mind was now in overdrive as a plan was forming. "It will not take Kenric long to realise that he has been duped and he will be after the true volume. He'll soon work out where it is. You must do as Ceolfrith asks and get there first Bede and prevent him getting his thieving hands on it." Hwaetberht was fired up and his plan was now becoming fully drawn as a he continued, "Take the second volume with you, as back up in case Kenric should usurp you. And as Ceolfrith suggested in his letter you must assume a false identity. Mmm....let me think...... I know.... collect some items or samples of glass from Tomas's glassworks. You can then pose as a merchant or better still a representative of the glassworks, attempting to win orders for the business. You can not obviously travel in your monk's habit. You should dress as a well to do merchant, not over flashy nor as dour as a peasant. I know of someone who fits your build, I'm sure that he will supply you with a suitable wardrobe. You have the education and the experience to carry it off and of course Kenric and his men have never met you and so will have no need to suspect anything if they come across you." He clasped his hands as if the enterprise was already accomplished and ushered me towards the door. As a parting thought he suggested that I ask Odin and Joseph to accompany me as additional protection. If they were agreeable then the monastery would recompense them and their families for the inconvenience.

So, next day, suitably attired as a well to do merchant with a box of Tomas's best products including drinking goblets, vases and samples of window glass, I left for Jarrow. Accompanied once again by Mika, bearing the burden of the Codex, we set off. But our journey would need to include a minor but crucial diversion.

$$* \qquad * \qquad * \qquad * \qquad * \qquad *$$

Primrose is a small hamlet near Jarrow and it is where both Joseph and Odin have settled with their families. We were welcomed with the usual hospitality and Mika was relieved of his duties, temporarily, whilst I met with my two long time friends. He was able to occupy himself with his cousin Lorenzo, talking about the forthcoming kickbladder tournament and soon a bladder was produced and off they went to an adjoining field to play.

I recounted the sad story of Ceolfrith once again, although bits and pieces of news had filtered their way, they were glad to hear it from the 'horse's mouth.' They were suitably grieved by news of the three deaths and were adamant that Ceolfrith's dying wishes should be fulfilled. Subject to the agreement of their wives, they declared they would be ready to travel the next day. As I was about to leave, my sister Gertrude joined our party and I had to, once again, avail her of the full details of what I had just told my two friends. They joined in whenever I missed or skipped an important point, as if they had been witness to the actual events. Gertrude nodded sagely when I explained the plan of action involving the reason for my current unorthodox attire. Something about Gertrude's stance and response to my account suggested that she was about to make a proposal and that I was not going to like it.

"I approve of Abbot Hwaetberht's plan but there is just one thing lacking in order to completely discourage this foul Kenric from suspecting your true identity. And that is......a woman!"

"A woman!" I cried in horror as if the very name of that sex was sufficient to court damnation. "What in the name of all that's good are you suggesting?"

"I am suggesting that a noble merchant should travel with a wife and that I should masquerade as that person. No one would suspect who you really are," I could see Joseph and Odin were absolutely bursting with mirth at the very idea and before I could command my thoughts sufficiently well to mount an objection, she went on. "Didn't Abraham our father in faith do much the same thing in the Old Testament?"

"No! Actually it was the other way round. He told people his wife was his sister! To protect her from predatory men." I corrected.

"Well it's the same idea. More or less. What do you two think about it?"

Those 'two' exploded with laughter and with choruses of 'Oo! you do make a lovely couple' ringing out. When they eventually settled down and after careful consideration they decided it actually was quite a good idea. Gertrude was intensely persuasive and I reluctantly agreed to her ruse. It was like when she was a child again and wanted to join in our games. I suppose we played so many tricks on her then that it is only fair I let her help now. She left our company after we all agreed to meet at Jarrow at dawn to begin our enterprise.

I found Mika and left Primrose to the smirks and grins of my two friends and arrived back at Jarrow soon after.

Chapter Twelve
The Investigation Begins

Joseph and Odin were invaluable and willing carriers of our luggage and glass samples, which enabled us to make quicker progress than if I and Gertrude had borne the burden. We travelled over land to the west coast and we picked up a knarr from near Carlisle. Based on the Viking longship, the knarr was built for speed and the transportation of cargo and not for the comfort of passengers. This was made all too plain to us as we boarded the ship and had to be satisfied with whatever makeshift accommodation we could find. Rudimentary beds were made on deck and tarpaulins acted as cover from the weather and night time cold. With a fair wind and, allied to the natural fast speed of the ship, we made even better time than Jean and Tomas had experienced on their return from France. So, after a couple of days of roughing it on board, we were glad to be set down on dry land at St. Nazaire in France where our friends had disembarked from their makeshift lifeboat. The knarr's ultimate destination was to be northern Spain so the captain was good enough to make a small detour to the French fishing village.

I have enough Norman French to get by and, after several enquiries of local fisher women, it enabled us to locate the graves of our two fallen friends and I led an impromptu service for the repose of their souls. Gertrude found some wild flowers with which she tenderly adorned their graves and we stood in quiet reflection for a number of minutes. Odin found some drift wood and, using his carpentry skills, made a cross and was able to etch out their names upon it. Chastened by this jolt of reality, regarding the circumstances surrounding our escapade, we determined to make Nantes before nightfall. Gertrude was a little too faithful in her new role as my spouse, paying much attention to me when we encountered strangers. She maintained that it was important to keep up the pretence, as we were never sure who was watching us. When we arrived at Nantes we took two rooms at an inn, needless to say I shared with Joseph and Odin whilst Gertrude had the benefit of the other room to herself. We took our evening repast in our rooms as we wished to maintain a low profile and not draw attention to ourselves.

Next morning we set about locating a livery stable where we would hire a horse and cart for the much longer leg of the journey to Langres, where our dear friend Ceolfrith's body lay. We took our luggage, samples and precious cargo with us. As we chatted to each other along the road, our discussions were interrupted by a deep voice speaking English with the hint of a Scottish accent.

"I thought I recognised that unmistakeable and unique northern twang that is betwixt Tyneside and Wearside! I haven't heard it since those halcyon days on Lindisfarne. My young friends from the Heb Burn, if I am not very much mistaken. And I thank God most high to see Odin here with us today, who I last saw sailing across the North Sea in a Viking longship."

We turned as one to see the welcome figure of our old dear friend Gregory, once a monk and now abbot of the monastery on Lindisfarne. We had heard of his rise but had never seen him since that visit to that holy isle many years ago. We let out exclamations of disbelief and warm embraces were exchanged and then enquires as to each others appearance in a French town. It was Gregory, the most senior of our group, who first offered his account.

"I am here on an errand of mercy, and I would guess that we may have a similar objective, for I am here to locate your own dear Abbot Ceolfrith. My travel companion is none other than Canon Kenric, assistant to His Eminence the Archbishop of Canterbury, our holy spiritual leader in England. The good Archbishop Bertwald had been informed of the shipwreck of the Angel of Northumbria when I was visiting him at Canterbury, on my way to Rome. He therefore seconded us to try to find survivors, if any. And bury the dead! Unfortunately we have been informed, by local inhabitants, of the death of two of the crew but we understand three survivors have made their way through this town and, presumably, on to Italy. I believe it was Ceolfrith's mission to take the Codex to our Holy Father in Rome when this tragic accident happened. A work of which I know you, Bede, have been much involved and has gained such notoriety within our Benedictine community. Ceolfrith was truly inspired by God to commission such an important work." Gregory paused for breath but from our facial expressions he could see that his account had not met with our total approval. I decided to intervene,

"Gregory! Ceolfrith is dead!"

It was Gregory's turn now to listen in silence as I unfurled the full details of Kenric's treachery. How the shipwreck was not accidental and the role of his henchman in Ceolfrith's sickness and the theft of the false codex. I concluded with news of Ceolfrith's resignation and contents of his dying letter and his wish to ensure safe delivery of the two true volumes, which accounted for our purpose here today. Gregory could only shake his head in disbelief at the deeds of his current travelling companion. He confessed that he disliked, almost instantly, the fawning Kenric but never thought him capable of such evil actions. He had seemed amiable enough on their travels together, feigning grief when they'd heard the news of Henry and Stephen's drowning. As my explanation drew to a close, Gregory seemed distant as if distracted by something, he nodded in the direction of the livery stable across the street.

"Look! Over there! It's him!" We turned in the direction he was nodding and saw the figure of Kenric walking towards two men who were carrying a similar satchel to that being carried by Joseph in our party. They came together in a huddle and then walked towards the barn. "They must be his henchmen you told me about and I suppose that satchel must contain the volume they think is the true Codex. Quick! Let's go to that alley next to the barn, the window is open and we may be able to see what's going on. But you must be quiet, we must not alert him."

We all followed Gregory across the road and hid in the alleyway behind some empty barrels. Through the window, and some gaps in the planking in the wall, we could just make out the outline of the three men. Kenric had laid the book on a bench and was carefully examining it. One of the men was talking to Kenric but his words were just an indistinguishable mumble to our ears. Kenric turned page after page, returning to earlier pages to re-examine the text. Then, suddenly and without warning, he exploded and this time the expletives and abuse that poured forth from his mouth were clearly audible and too strong for me to repeat here. Gertrude blushed with embarrassment and the two lads stuffed their fingers into their mouths to stifle a reaction. Gregory raised his eyes to the sky and the fake volume could be seen flying through the air of the barn. Gregory took advantage of the cacophony to half mouth and half whisper,

"I think he's discovered it's the false codex." As the stream of invective continued, we took the opportunity to leave the alleyway and Gregory, who was familiar with the town, told us of another livery stable at the other end of Nantes and in the direction of our travel. He suggested we hire our cart and steed from there and leave forthwith for Langres. He would delay his and Kenric's departure, in order to give us a head start. We arranged to meet again in a few days time in the Church of the Twin Martyrs at Langres. As we took our leave of Gregory we could hear that Kenric was still in full flow, berating his two agents, and I understood the meaning of that old saying about turning the air blue!

*   *   *   *   *   *

Gertrude has lost none of her ability to complain and, I don't know if it was seeing Gregory again, the journey to Langres reminded me of the time we all went to Lindisfarne so long ago. I remember her complaining so much about the few times she had to walk to save the donkey, that my father would lift her gently onto the cart and tell her she had 'done her bit.' Once again at least two of us would walk in order to give the four legged beast some relief but I think she sat on top of the cart, regal like, for most of the miles from Nantes to Langres. We arrived at Langres as the light was fading and we decided we would rest up for the night before seeking the remains of our deceased friend. This concession to our fatigue must have allowed Gregory and his party to catch up with us, though they never overtook us on the road.

But when we arrived at the Church of the Twin Martyrs next day, there Gregory stood at the lych gate waiting our arrival. Lych gates are porticos or shelters where the funeral pall bearers wait, with the corpse, for the clergyman to arrive. The corpse we wanted to see was not resting at the gate but in the cold crypt beneath the nave of the church. The reason for our friend's terse greeting was soon apparent to us from his explanation.

"Quickly, we haven't much time. Kenric has gone first to Gangulphus' monastery to pay his respects before coming here. He is bishop and overseerer of the parish and Kenric is a stickler for formality. I gave my excuses on some pretext of business in town so that I could meet you before he arrives. Let's go down to the crypt."

Both Joseph and Odin said that they would rather stay and guard the Codex and luggage. They wished to remember Ceolfrith as he was when alive and preferred not to see his corpse. Gregory said they could alert us in the crypt if Kenric arrived unexpectedly. He suggested they rang the lych bell which sat on a bench inside the gate. This was rung at funerals to herald the arrival of the priest, who may not be resident in the parish, as often the corpse could rest for several days in the lych gate awaiting his arrival. The mourners alerted by the bell would then assemble for the funeral.

The two nodded their understanding and Gregory, Gertrude and I approached the church. After descending the steep stone staircase of the crypt we saw the body of our friend shrouded in white linen and lying on a stone bed. He seemed to be the sole resident of the crypt although there were three or four empty stone slabs awaiting occupants. The room was icy cold and, together with the holiness of our beloved Abbot Ceolfrith, had helped preserve his body. We instinctively knelt in a time of quiet prayer. I then led us in the De Profundis with Gertrude and Gregory responding:

Out of the depths I have cried to Thee O Lord! Lord, hear my voice.
Let Thine ears be attentive to the voice of my supplication.
If Thou, O Lord! Wilt mark iniquities: Lord, who shall stand it?
For with Thee there is mercy: and by reason of Thy law I have waited on
Thee, O Lord!
My soul hath relied on His word: my soul hath hoped in the Lord.
From the morning watch even until night: let Israel hope in the Lord.
For with the Lord there is mercy; and with Him plentiful Redemption.

And He will redeem Israel from all his iniquities.
Eternal rest give unto him, O Lord!
And let perpetual light shine upon him.
May he rest in peace.
Amen.

Lord, hear my prayer.
And let my cry come unto Thee.
Bless, O my God! the repose I am about to take, that, renewing my
strength, I may be better enabled to serve Thee. Pour down Thy blessings,
O Lord! on my parents, relations, friends, and enemies. Protect the Pope,
our bishop, and all the pastors of Thy holy Church. Assist the poor and the
afflicted, and those who are now in their last agony. Look with an eye of
pity on thy servant Ceolfrith; and lead him forth into everlasting joy.

Gregory was the first to rise and he drew nearer the body and seemed to be examining his face in great detail. We gasped as Gregory pulled up Ceolfrith's eyelids which had been closed upon his death. Then he did the same to his mouth and Gertrude could take it no longer and let out an exclamation.

"It's alright I know what I am doing." he whispered with a form of reverence which now seemed incongruous after his rough handling of the cadaver. "I don't have my scientific equipment with me and I can not be one hundred percent sure but....." I looked at my sister, her brow furrowed confusedly. "From his dilated pupils and the dryness of the mouth I would say there are effects of atropa belladonna!"

"What!.....You m..mean..." I stuttered, mouth open incredulously.

"He means what?" demanded Gertrude growing impatient at being the only one not to follow Gregory's train of thought.

"Deadly nightshade Gertrude." replied Gregory. "Which means Ceolfrith could have been.... I say could have been.... well I mean, I have no proof but...Ceolfrith could have been.... poisoned!"

We were both now speechless, as the impact of Gregory's words sunk in. We knew that Kenric had no compunction in killing our two young friends, or certainly ordering their deaths, but Jean and Tomas had not raised the possibility that Ceolfrith's death could be foul play. He had been ill as a result of the inclement weather and the two had presumed that his death was from natural causes. Although the evidence was inconclusive and circumstantial, it nevertheless fitted with the profile of such a ruthless man. Obviously, he had not actually performed the deed himself, his type seldom do, they rarely incriminate themselves. But it was probable that Kenric was behind Ceolfrith's death and this made their mission all the more hazardous.

Gregory now turned his attention to the box which lay at the feet of Ceolfrith's body. The lock was broken and he opened the lid to find Ceolfrith's habit amongst his personal effects. Gregory examined the box with his usual scientific precision from both the inside and the outer casing. He drew our attention to the discrepancy in depth from one to the other and, after further poking and prodding, he discovered the hinge for the false bottom which he opened to reveal the Codex. Carefully he lifted it from its hidden home and placed it upon one of the empty slabs. Gregory examined it in awe and admiration.

"Bede. This is wonderful, a true work of art and a glorification of God our Creator." I felt the sin of pride rise once again in my breast and, convicted by the holiness of my surroundings, mentally confessed this to my Lord. I suggested that we lose no further time and transport it, together with its sister volume sitting outside on the cart, with all expediency to Rome. But Gregory had other ideas.

"No Bede my good friend I think not." I could see that Gregory was mulling over the most efficacious course of action we should take. "No! Kenric will not be assuaged by the volume not being here when he arrives. He will assume that it has been taken and follow in hot pursuit. He is not without contacts and agents willing to do his bidding. This may lead him to discover the existence of the second copy. Have you got your maps with you? The ones which plot your route to Rome?"

Gertrude anticipated my request to find them and quickly returned from the cart with our detailed maps. Gregory laid them open on another vacant slab. He pointed at the maps in a way which demanded my attention.

"I want you to make your way across France to this village of Chamonix on the Swiss border and ask for Didier," said Gregory who had travelled extensively throughout France and indeed the whole of Europe and it was we who were now to be the beneficiaries of his knowledge and contacts. "He will lead you through the mountains to Italy. He will take you the quickest way possible. It is arduous but you all have the youth and health to cope with it. Meanwhile I will travel with Kenric, with the other Codex, on a more circuitous route suitable for men of our age."

Gregory looked satisfied with his suggestion but could see that I required further elucidation. He realised that he now had my implicit agreement and continued.

"I want you to take your volume to a safe house I know here." He pointed to an area in northern Italy in the region of Toscana. "Here up a mountain is the Abbey of the Saviour and you must ask for Abbot Peter. He is an old man who has many years in the service of the Gospel and the furtherance of the Kingdom of God. He can be trusted completely. You will leave your volume in safety there and rendezvous with me in Rome. Your route through the Alps will give you three, possibly four days advantage on us. Sufficient time to make the diversion and press on to Rome."

Gregory's instructions had been delivered at a breathless rate and I managed to interject one short question.

"But what about your journey? Kenric's henchmen can not be far away. Isn't it dangerous?"

"Kenric will be satisfied with the honour of escorting the volume for now. It will appeal to his sense of self importance. You must avoid the large Italian cities of Turin, Milan and Florence and use the more rural routes. I will suggest we visit these cities and I will allow Kenric to display the Codex himself to all the worthy citizens. No doubt he will try to pass it off as his work. He will make a move but I think it will be nearer to Rome. I will be prepared for him when he does so. Do not worry. I came to Lindisfarne from Iona, from a family of Picts. I tell you they can give any man alive a run for his money. When you come to write your history, Bede, be sure to include something about the Picts."

Before Gregory could wax lyrical any more about his ancestry, the sound of a bell could be heard in the distance. The pre-arranged signal announcing Kenric's imminent arrival.

"Kenric!" exclaimed Gregory who reminded us that he was unaware of our identity and would be too pre-occupied with the Codex to worry about us. This seemed to be confirmed as the canon swept into the crypt, seemingly oblivious to our existence. Seeing the body of Ceolfrith I swear crocodile tears flowed like a waterfall from the duplicitous cleric, who addressed the body.

"My dear brother in Christ. How I am saddened at the sight of your incorruptible body before me." He took a kerchief from his habit and dabbed his eyes and, like an actor on the stage, sought his adoring audience. Noticing that his travelling companion had been joined by two strangers he looked quizzically at Gregory and then addressed me directly,

"Sir, I am at a disadvantage to whom am I addressing?"

"Eh.......Edwin, my name is Edwin." Not an untruth, as I am indeed named after my late father and Edwin is my middle name. Then turning to Gertrude I said, "And this is my kinswoman." Again not an untruth as, although I could see Kenric assumed we were married, the appellation kinswoman could also include a sister. "We are glass merchants from Monkwearmouth in Northumbria and we wished to pay our respects to our much mourned abbot and parish priest." I consoled myself with the thought that glass merchant was technically correct at the moment but was stretching the truth a little. I could see that Gregory was pleased with my extemporary explanation as Kenric replied,

"Ah yes I have just returned from Gangulphus who has appraised me of the full facts of our lord Ceolfrith's untimely demise. He had been gladly received by the lord of this region who had previously met Ceolfrith on the way and invited him to come and stay with him and assured him of a warm welcome. Gangulphus urgently pressed him not to depart until he was well or if God so willed it, to await his entry into the life of heaven by the tombs of the holy martyrs. Sadly he died on the very day he arrived at about the tenth hour. On the next day, with a great company of believers he was brought the three miles from Gangulphus' monastery to his resting place here." Kenric was in his element adding totally fallacious details to his account of Ceolfrith's death. Details which failed to include his own role in that death. He would have proceeded at even greater length had not his attention been distracted by the open volume on the stone slab. "Ah....I see you have discovered the holy Codex which had been so cruelly arrested on its journey to Rome. I knew it must be with Ceolfrith's body."

With Kenric's focus now fully on the beautiful volume of scripture, Gregory took the opportunity to suggest that we take our leave and proceed on our way. We bade adieu to Canon Kenric but he was so lost in concentration that he could barely lift an arm in recognition of our farewell. Gregory ushered us out of the crypt and whispered reminders of our earlier discussions. He embraced us and reassured us that all would be well and that the Spirit of God was the inspiration and protector of our venture.

Before too long we were making haste on our long journey across France to seek Didier our guide and the spire of the Church of the Twin Martyrs ebbed slowly from our sight.

Chapter Thirteen
Didier

Days of tedium ensued as we trudged across country, stopping off periodically to rest overnight and exchange our horse for a fresh one at various livery stables. We had been supplied with a generous amount of gold from Abbot Hwaetberht which we were able to exchange for local currency. I was rather embarrassed to barter with the locals but Gertrude was more forthright and ensured that we received a fair exchange for our precious metal. I was initially responsible for carrying this treasure but Gertrude had the sensible idea of dividing it between us for security purposes. Ironically we have not felt threatened on our tour other than the implicit threat from where none should exist; from our own Christian kinsmen Kenric and his associates! My rudimentary French was constantly put to the test and I struggled to cope with the various dialects, which sometimes sounded almost like a different language. Eventually though I was successful enough to gain directions to our destination of Chamonix and further enquiries led us to the homestead of Didier. The small holding reminded me a little of my childhood home at the Heb Burn and I could see that this had evoked the same feelings in my sister.

"Bede, I think we are home," she said smiling warmly, "I fully expect to hear mam shouting Edwin! Edwin! I am sure I can see Bridget doing some washing over there."

She could indeed see a young girl, resembling our sister, twisting some linen cloth in order to wring out as much moisture as possible before beating it senseless on a large stone. I interrupted her to inquire about the whereabouts of her father who, I presumed, was Didier the man we had been instructed to find. It seemed my assumption was correct as she disappeared inside and a small hairy man came out and bounded towards us. I quickly appraised him of the recommendation from Gregory, his acquaintance, and asked if he was available for hire to help navigate us through the dangers of the Alps. He stood listening attentively to my request and visibly reacted to the mention of our dear mutual friend's name. He shook me warmly by the hand.

"You come well recommended my friends," said Didier, "for I would not embark on such a dangerous escapade unless my good friend Gregory had sent you. For I am an old man now and seldom walk the mountains which can easily claim the lives of those unwitting travellers but I owe him the life of my own dear daughter, the young girl you see before you now. Since my wife died she is the only family I have and she is worth more to me than life itself."

He looked fondly at the girl who was now hanging the washing on a line to dry. "Once when Gregory was travelling to Italy, he was diverted to my home. I swear it was by God's good grace. For it just so happened that my daughter, Teresa, had contracted a fever and lay dying. Hope had all but deserted me when that holy man knocked upon my door to ask for directions."

The memory of his daughter, lying sick at the entrance to death was proving painful for Didier and he bit his lower lip, determined that he would conclude his story without breaking down into tears.

"Seeing my daughter's predicament he read me a passage from the letter of James in the New Testament. I remember the words well for I have committed them to memory and hold them in my heart. *Is anyone among you sick? Let them call the elders of the church to pray over them and anoint them with oil in the name of the Lord.* Gregory turned to me and told me that he was indeed that elder and he proceeded to anoint her and command the fever to leave her in the name of Jesus Christ. The fever burnt even fiercer than it had done and he cursed the fever once again and commanded Satan to release my daughter from his oppression, as the blood of Jesus had redeemed her and by His wounds she was healed. He later told me that it was the Lord Jesus himself who said that we should speak to the mountains and command them to move. You only have to take a look around you here to see the mountains to understand how the words of the Lord mean so much. Now you see my daughter in good health. I know it was by the power of God she was healed but it was Gregory who was the means of God's grace and I will always be grateful to him. Any friend of Gregory will always be welcome at Didier's home in the village of Chamonix. Come my friends and share our meal. Teresa! Come and meet some friends of Gregory."

Teresa, who had remained shyly in the background, grew more confident at the sound of Gregory's name and she came forward to greet our party. Gertrude and Odin helped Teresa prepare our evening meal whilst Joseph cut some wood for the fire. I talked with Didier about our situation and I appraised him in detail of all the events which had taken place and why four strangers from the north east of England were wandering the foothills of the Alps. I unfurled our map and pointed to our next destination of Abbazia di San Salvatore (The Abbey of the Saviour). It was at Gregory's express instruction that we were heading for this abbey. Didier stroked his beard thoughtfully, scrunching his nose a few times as if mentally dismissing a particular route in favour of another. However, he obviously felt unable to disclose his favoured course until he was absolutely sure. Then after much deliberation he seemed certain enough to share his findings with me.

"So, your intention is to get to here in Tuscany." He pointed to the mountainous area where the abbey was situated and as if to confirm our wishes before committing himself he continued, "You want to go by the quickest route possible, irrespective of the degree of difficulty and you are sure that you are all fit enough to withstand the trek?" Having assured himself that we met all his criteria, he disclosed the route whilst referring to the map and pointing the same to me. "First day we will walk along the Chamonix Valley to Trient in Switzerland which, if you are as fit as you say you are, should take about seven or eight hours. Second day the journey from Trient to Champex should take about the same time. These first two days will be as nothing to the third when we transfer to Ferret and ascend to the Grand Col Ferret path and on into Italy. Finally on day four we will descend into northern Italy where I will leave you to continue your journey. We will take provisions for four days and will spend the nights bivouacking in the open air. As the year is drawing to its autumn the evenings will be cold. I will supply warm blankets for the bivouac but we must travel as lightweight as possible." He looked accusingly at our luggage sat quietly in the corner.

"I appreciate what you say Didier." I replied, "We have no further need for the subterfuge of travelling incognito. Perhaps you could make use of the glassware samples we have brought? That is the bulk of our luggage but of course the Codex must travel with us" Didier graciously accepted the samples which he thought he could put to good use and we agreed a fee for his services. That evening we enjoyed the hospitality of our newly made friends and Didier regaled us with hair raising stories of hazardous treks through the Alps. I think he saw that the colour was draining from our faces but he managed to rescue the situation with good humour and assurances that we would be accompanied by the most sure footed guide in France – himself! He advised that we retire early for the night as we would require all our energy in the next few days.

*   *   *   *   *   * *

When I looked at the map, Didier's planned route seemed counter intuitive as we seemed to be walking away from the direction of Italy. However our map took no consideration of the erratic terrain and this is where his experience proved invaluable. By taking a seemingly tortuous route we were in fact using the geographical features to our advantage. The end result, although exhausting, would give us the extra time required to safely deposit our Codex with the trustworthy monks at Monte Amiata and then enable us to arrive in Rome in good time. Didier had combed through the Alps for all his adult life and most of his childhood. Like a mountain goat he had picked his way carefully over scree and had rejected too dangerous paths for safer ones. These safe routes had been committed to memory and additional knowledge had been passed down to him from his father and added to and improved upon by his own experience.

The early autumn morning was a glorious testament to the Creator's work as we ambled our way through the valley, each of us carrying our bedding and Joseph and Odin taking turns carrying the bulky satchel containing the Codex. Ahead of us stood the awe inspiring Monte Blanc, capped with pure white snow. It overlooked the valley like a beneficent parent taking an intimate interest in the ant like people going about their business on foot and in boats upon the river. It kept secret the many men and women lost upon its slopes, creatures less adapted for the environment than the goats and sheep which frolicked unselfconsciously, as their betters lay frozen in death. Some would be recovered but those bodies which had fallen in more precarious positions were left to decay and provide food for the scavenging animals. Didier, ropes draped around his torso, allowed us to walk at our own pace in the knowledge that we were keeping to the time he had allowed for the journey. Almost to the minute of his prediction, we arrived at our first check point of Trient, a small village further up the valley and the mountain. It was a tribute to Didier's gentle introduction to our exertions that we had not noticed that we had climbed several thousand feet from Chamonix. Although we did not know it at the time, our camp for the first evening of our walk was quite luxurious. Luxurious compared with what was to come. A small barn, belonging to a contact of Didier, provided a rudimentary hotel for us. After a sparse meal of bread and cheese we bedded down for the night. The straw provided a soft mattress as we snuggled beneath our blankets. Calves were also nestling down to sleep in stalls across from us and Gertrude remarked how like a nativity scene we all were. After stories and laughter in the dark, we were reprimanded like naughty school children by Didier and, eventually, we settled down.

Next day we left Trient for Champex and almost immediately we noticed a pull on our leg muscles, as the incline increased in strength. Thankfully the paths were well beaten and in good order, with only the odd rock to impede our progress. High up in the Swiss Alps, Champex Lac is a picturesque lakeside hamlet surrounded by woods. We made camp by the lake and Gertrude and Odin decided to chance their fishing skills in the shallow waters of the tarn. Odin, proud of his Viking fishing ancestry, was orchestrating proceedings. Joseph said he would look for wood and have a fire blazing in time to grill the catch. Odin knew he had thrown down the gauntlet and it was now a matter of honour that he deliver a supplement to the supplies Didier had so generously provided. Gertrude's role was purely advisory as her knowledge of fishing was totally theoretical. This didn't prevent her from directing operations with her strident instructions echoing through the mountain scenery. After several abortive attempts, Odin managed to succeed in catching two substantially sized bream, much to the surprise of Joseph who had managed to start a conflagration, which he thought would be used to provide us with warmth rather than a means of cooking.

We all welcomed this excellent supplement to our diet and I reminded everyone of the parsnip chips which Gregory had made for us on Lindisfarne. Apart from the loss of Odin, I think we all remembered our time on Lindisfarne and visit to Inner Farne with fondness. As dusk closed in over the lake, and the mountains took on a more sinister shadowy appearance, I recalled the mysterious apparition I had experienced on Inner Farne and at the well near the Heb Burn. These experiences of the spiritual still remain a vivid reminiscence. We get glimpses of the eternal during our lifetime and they should be treasured and kept close to our heart. As darkness fell, so the coldness began to bite and there was less light-hearted banter than the night before. Joseph had provided a plentiful supply of wood and we agreed that, whoever was awake would feed the camp fire during the night. This proved an easy task, as our rest was one of constant interruption and fitful sleep and as a result the fire rarely flagged.

Although our night had lacked sleep, at least we greeted the dawn with warm bodies and breakfasted on bread. Didier introduced us to a new take on it by skewering some bread on a stick and holding it close to the fire. The bread changed to a golden brown colour and before it started to burn he withdrew it from the fire. He called this toast and said it was a good way to use stale bread. It was crisp and hot and Joseph said it might be better with some butter or cheese on it. We gathered our belongings and Joseph and Odin ensured that the fire, which had heated us so loyally during the night, was fully extinguished. They doused the embers with cool crystal water from the lake and then refilled the gourds with the refreshing liquid for our day's journey. This was to be the most physically arduous and technically difficult we had encountered and Didier told us to prepare ourselves accordingly.

"Friends! Today we will encounter many hazards and rough passage. Many of the pathways I know will have been washed away or rock falls may block our way. You all MUST listen to my instructions and do exactly what I ask you to do. Like all good Christians we will keep to the straight and narrow path."

With this allusion to the Gospel words he invited us to begin our trek. So far the ropes circumnavigating Didier's body had been only decorative but today they would be used in earnest and our lives would literally depend upon them. As if he had some crystal ball or means of predicting the future his words proved true very soon. We had to clamber up the sides of scree slopes and walk along knife edge arêtes with valleys falling away from us on both sides. A fall would surely kill the unwary trekker, no doubt after their body had been mangled and torn on the pointed rocks below. We needed the calm and reassuring voice of Didier to inspire confidence in us, as we slowly picked our way, step by step, along the ridges. Having succeeded in conquering each death defying obstacle we were relentlessly presented with a succession of even greater trials. Periodically we stopped as one, to rest and take swigs of the refreshing lake water. No one said a word and anxious looks were exchanged. The realisation came upon us that we had come too far to change our minds, even if that were a realistic option. The dangers in returning to our lakeside camp were balanced out by the unknown ones which we could only anticipate were to come. This resulted in a kind of mental paralysis in me and I suddenly felt that this was going to manifest itself physically. I was at the rear of the party as my friends tentatively moved off. I found myself rooted to the spot and I spread my arms against the wall of rock behind me in an attempt to anchor my body. I was in a state of panic and I called out.

"Help! Help! I don't think I can move," I said. My words repeated themselves in an echo of accusation. Didier raised his hand to arrest the progress of the rest of the group. He invited them to move on and carefully pass by him and then he returned to me. He took a rope from around his body and fed it around my waist and knotted it securely at my stomach. He then took the other end of the rope and did the same around his waist.

"Bede." he whispered, "I have secured you to me. Should you slip then I will be able to break your fall. But I assure you you are not going to fall. Bede, remember the words of the psalmist -*The LORD directs the steps of the godly. He delights in every detail of their lives. Though they stumble, they will never fall, for the LORD holds them by the hand. You have made a wide path for my feet to keep them from slipping."*

I felt ashamed of my lack of faith and for not relying on the Word of God in my predicament. I was thankful for the inspirational words uttered by our guide. I recalled that someone, it may well have been Ceolfrith, once told me when I was fearful to remember a mnemonic for the word fear – **F**alse **E**xpectations **A**ppearing **R**eal.

I stepped out hesitantly, holding the rope with my right hand and the wall of rock with my left. All the while I repeated the verses of the psalm under my breath and the reassuring words buoyed me up. Didier backed away from me ensuring the tension of the rope was sufficient to assure me and then, when he thought I was feeling more confident, he nodded and turned in the direction of travel. Thirty minutes or so later we reached a safe clearing where I received slaps and hugs of reassurance from the rest of the group. They all said they had similar feelings and seeing what happened to me had helped them overcome their fears. The clearing proved a vantage point for us to survey our achievements and see that we had overcome the most treacherous impediments. Didier however interrupted our self congratulatory discussions to warn us about complacency for the final part of the journey. He told us that more lives had been lost here than on top of the mountain. Concentration levels were highest at the most perilous points but fatigue and a false sense of security had undermined them on their descent and consequently they had paid the ultimate penalty. We took one last opportunity to take in the panorama and vista and I offered up a prayer of praise and thanksgiving for our expedition so far and for a safe conclusion to our day.

We each picked up our blankets and prepared to make our way down the mountain with Didier's cautioning uppermost in our minds. Odin took over the responsibility of carrying the Codex from Joseph, who chided his friend for his lack of contribution to the cause of transporting the load. Odin rose to the bait and protested his innocence and catalogued the numerous times he had carried it. Joseph smiled and patted Odin, patronisingly, on the back and chalked it down to another wind up won. The holy volume had been a silent witness to our endeavours and sat secure and snug in its leather satchel. I thought about the work which had gone into it and wondered whether it was worth the loss of two lives and possibly more, if Kenric had his way.

Thanks be to God we descended in safety and as it was late in the day Didier decided to spend one last night with us bivouacking, before returning the way we had come. I shuddered inwardly at the thought of the reverse journey and thanked God again that I would not have to undertake it. I think I am as bad a mountaineer as I am sailor! Once again Didier's network of contacts proved useful and we spent the evening in the comparative comfort of a barn.

Chapter Fourteen
Abbazia di San Salvatore
(The Abbey of the Saviour)

Fog shrouded our first morning in northern Italy. Mist swirled down from the mountains, their caps of snow now hidden from view by the grey watery vapour and obscuring the path that we had used only yesterday and, which would have to be picked out by our faithful guide on his return to Chamonix upon leaving us. Before beginning the next section of our journey Didier prevailed upon his friend to supply us with a hearty breakfast of ham, cheese and bread washed down with milk, a welcome boost to our energy levels for our forthcoming walk. When we had finished, Didier laid out our map on the table and traced our route to Monte Amiata.

"Keep to these roads, to the west of the big cities and you should be all right. Break your journey here," he said, his rough gnarled finger pointing to a promontory to the north of a small lake called Orta, next to several larger ones. "There are many bigger lakes nearby, Como, Maggiore and Garda but the towns around them will be well populated and Gregory's advice was to avoid too much contact with the locals." I thought that this was rather unsociable of us but sensible. Now that we had dropped the pretence of being merchants and our sole purpose was to deliver the Codex, news of our ulterior motive may spread and arouse the interest of Kenric and his network of informants. We wished to keep as low a profile as possible and not attract any attention. Didier now concluded his travelogue, "You will be getting tired by the time you get here and you can pay for a sculler to row you down the lake, to save your feet. In the middle of the lake is an island called Isola San Guilio. Stay for the night at the tiny monastery there; you are safe to disclose your true identity to Brother Giuseppe, a hermit who is the only person to live on the island. Mention that Didier sent you and he will make you feel at home. He will show you the unique devotion he has. I'll not spoil it for you but you will find it most uplifting." Didier neatly folded our map as if his instructions needed no further elucidation. He then passed the folded document to Gertrude. I was intrigued by his final comments which filled me with great anticipation for the day ahead and wondered what the unique devotion could be. The final flourish of the map folding heralded his farewell and, after much hugging and promises to meet again some day, we took our leave.

Our chosen route was probably more arduous than the main, more crowded, thoroughfares which may have attracted inquisitive strangers and increased the danger of Kenric being alerted. The late autumn/early winter morning was warm and we toiled, barely speaking, for most of the day.

We eventually arrived at the north end of Lago di Orta, a long thin waterway interrupted by a tree clad island, which we assumed to be Isola San Guilio. This assumption was confirmed by a middle aged man sitting in a large row boat mending fishing nets. I was able to communicate with him using Latin. The locals speak their own dialect of Latin which is becoming to be known as Italian but I haven't quite mastered the nuances of it yet. I made my meaning known to him and after clicking his teeth he replied,

"Is Brother Giuseppe expecting you?" he asked tersely. "He doesn't usually accept visitors. I take provisions out to him now and then and he barely grunts at me!" It was obvious that this lack of hospitality irked the sculler and, the thought of strangers receiving a warmer welcome than he did, was not pleasing to him. I informed him that we had all been well recommended to him, and the occupant of the island, by our new friend Didier and this declaration was like a key unlocking the door of a strong box. "Didier! Why didn't you say. Come on hop in. Just as well you are travelling light. I've just enough room for you all as passengers together with that bag. Any more and I would have to have made two journeys."

I would not have liked to have trespassed upon his good nature and was glad that we virtually travelled in the clothes we wore. The blankets had been donated to Didier's friend at our previous stop, as neither he nor us could have carried them. They would invariably find a use by the numerous passing travellers that frequented that Alpine route.

We glided into a natural harbour on the island and our pilot yelled out our arrival to the sole inhabitant, dropping Didier's name into the explanation, and the good brother scurried from an undergrowth of bushes to meet us. Introductions were made (using my true identity) and arrangements made with the sculler to be collected the following morning.

We followed Brother Giuseppe up a steep path to a clearing with the smallest chapel I had ever seen, next to a building obviously used as his residence. We were welcomed into a deceptively large room with a table and two benches. A fire burned in the hearth and I could see, through an open door, the monk's bedroom. A meal was hastily prepared and he diligently waited on us until we were replete. The embers of the fire glowed as he poked it with a stick and then fed it with a clod of peat. He suggested that Gertrude take his bed for the night and that the four males sleep in the small chapel. Gertrude made an attempt at protestation but I knew she was hoping that this would be declined, as she preferred the comfort and warmth of the small cottage to a dusty, draughty chapel. Her hope was realised as we trooped into the dingy stone building. Brother Giuseppe and I took turns to read the evening Divine Office and we all settled down, tired from our days walk and slept surprisingly sound.

Next morning I asked Brother Giuseppe about the devotion Didier had referred to. He said that if we had time he would show us it and so we all assembled, eager to hear what he had to say.

"My devotion is to the cross upon which our Saviour Jesus died," he said and I could sense his deep reverence and zeal for his subject. "We fail to realise, fully, exactly what actually took place on that Good Friday upon Golgotha Hill, those hundreds of years ago. We must meditate deeply on these sacred mysteries and I have devised this help or aid to our meditations."

He went on to tell us that he had carved small scenes from Jesus' passion and death, tracing the route from His condemnation to His death on the cross at Calvary. Figures were fashioned out of wood and had been rudely painted in vivid colours. Each one had a Roman numeral above it, denoting the chronology of Jesus' passion from one to fourteen. As he took us around the island, to look at the episodes, he gave a small homily by way of explanation.

"Some of the scenes are directly from the scriptures and some I have added to from my own imagination of what I think may have happened, which I hope has been inspired by prayer and the Holy Spirit. At each scene we will stop and remain stationary and reflect upon what it means. Therefore I have called each stop a station. The devotion is known as the Stations of the Cross."

We stood in silent appreciation of Brother Giuseppe's explanation and we waited in expectation for him to show us the stations. He waved his right hand indicating that he wished us to follow.

"I. The first station is - Pilate condemns Jesus to die. Pilate knew that Jesus was innocent, yet he literally washed his hands of all responsibility. The crowd of Jews was not placated and so he thought he had a way out and offered to release Jesus or a notorious criminal called Barabbas. He was actually called Jesus Barabbas (which means son of Abba, meaning father). So the crowd were presented with the real Jesus and a false Jesus. They chose the false Jesus!"

We stood and reflected on this scene and how we, like that baying crowd, often choose the false Jesus in our lives. The scriptures tell us that there will be many Christs and Antichrists and we must stay true to the real one so that we are not led astray. I had never thought of that distinction between the two men called Jesus in the condemnation episode from the Gospels, although I had read it many times; already Giuseppe's devotion was having an affect on me. He led us to the next station and continued,

"II. The second station - Jesus accepts His cross. After beating Him with whips and pressing a crown of thorns into His head the soldiers made Jesus carry His own means of execution to the gallows. Jesus says, unless we carry our own crosses we can NOT be His followers. But sometimes people carry the wrong cross. Crosses of sickness and unhappiness are not the true cross. God our Father never wishes sickness and unhappiness on us; as Jesus said, *Which of you fathers, if your son asks for a fish, will give him a snake instead?* God our Father wants us to be well and happy. Jesus means that we must carry the cross of being a Christian and that means dying to everything that this world holds dear! It means suffering ridicule and injustice on behalf of the Gospel. *Be glad when someone mocks you and persecutes you on my behalf.*"

Moving some two hundred yards around the island we come to the third station, Giuseppe clears his throat before beginning his explanation.

"III. The third station – Jesus falls for the first time. Already weak from the beating he had endured and the loss of blood, Jesus stumbles and falls. Though he is without sin his stumble is physical. But we who are sinful, and may even believe in Jesus, often stumble and fall away from his teaching. Jesus does not condemn us when we stumble; we must repent and receive forgiveness for our sins."

In the time of silent reflection we all ask forgiveness for our sins, as we move to the next station.

"IV. The fourth station – Jesus meets His mother Mary. His mother was with Him all the way to the cross. Mary must have remembered the words of Simeon when Jesus was a baby. A temple official, Simeon prophesied that a sword would piece her heart. Mary questioned God when the news of Jesus birth came to her from Gabriel. She asked *'How can this be for I am virgin?'* Her questioning of God was positive – how can this be? She would need all the faith of God to ask Him – how can Jesus overcome this? But she never lost faith; even in the darkest moments and we too must remember that the stars shine only in darkness."

As we move on to the next stop the sun glints on the waters of the lake.

"V. The fifth station - Simon helps carry the cross. Simon of Cyrene was press-ganged into helping Jesus. He was an observer, he did not volunteer but what a privilege he was given to share Jesus' suffering in a small way. Sometimes we may be asked to carry a cross not meant for us. A cross of confusion and misunderstanding but be assured that you can cast that burden upon Jesus who will bear it even unto death. He asks us to carry the cross, like Simon, for only a short distance."

Odin and Joseph lead us to the next station which they have discovered attached to an old oak tree.

"VI. The sixth station - Veronica wipes the face of Jesus. I have imagined that one of the many women, who followed and supported Jesus, wiped His face as a sign of compassion. Perhaps it was the woman who thought she only had to touch the hem of His garment to be healed and whose faith was rewarded with an instant cure. I have called her Veronica, from the Greek meaning true image. I have imagined that the face of Jesus would be imprinted upon the cloth. But of course it would be the reverse image of His face, so not quite a true image. So I believe we should not venerate icons and images of Jesus. No! Rather we should venerate the true face of Jesus - His Word, which we read in the scriptures and put those words into practice. Otherwise we will be as the apostle James says - *someone who sees their face in the mirror and forgets it.*"

As we reach the half way point of our devotion Gertrude loses her footing and Giuseppe stretches out his arm to steady her.

"VII. The seventh station – Jesus falls a second time. Even without carrying the cross Jesus is so weak that he falls a second time."

The figure which Giuseppe has carved is so moving, seeing Jesus prostrate with the cross, carried by Simon, overshadowing Him. Giuseppe carries on.

"VIII. The eighth station – Jesus meets the women of Jerusalem. It seems it is only the women who are brave enough to support Jesus in his trials. The apostles have deserted him and Judas has betrayed him. They cry out in sorrow, weeping for the man they see so ill used. But he tells them not to weep for Him rather '*weep for yourselves and for your children. For the time will come when you will say, 'Blessed are the childless women, the wombs that never bore and the breasts that never nursed. For if people do these things when the tree is green, what will happen when it is dry?'* A harrowing warning."

Gertrude has that self satisfied look which I have seen so often when she has berated me about the role of women in the Church. I know precisely what she is thinking; that it is women who have been the mainstay of our faith for centuries. Our host gently invites us on.

"IX. The ninth station – Jesus falls for the third time. Peter denied Jesus three times and so fell three times. But Jesus, after he rises from death, asks Peter three times if he loves Him. Peter does not fall this time. No matter how many times we fall, forgiveness is only a prayer away".
I recall Godric telling me that it is easy to forgive until someone does something to you that requires forgiveness!

"X. The tenth station – Jesus is stripped of His clothes. To fulfil the prophecy of the Psalms, *They divide my clothes among them and cast lots for my garment.* Jesus is humiliated by the Roman soldiers, yet he did not utter any reproach. We too, as part of the cross we carry, may be required to suffer humiliation in the world's eyes. For, what we believe in will not be popular with those who are being lost. We too should, like Jesus, turn the other cheek"

When we get to the next point we see that Giuseppe has depicted the full horror of Jesus' crucifixion and his explanation is more deliberate and sensitive.

"XI. The eleventh station – Jesus is nailed to the cross. His hands and His feet are torn by the iron nails, as He is fixed to the cross. The prophesy of Isaiah is fulfilled, *But he was pierced for our transgressions, he was crushed for our iniquities; the punishment that brought us peace was on him, and by his wounds we are healed.* This is another far reaching benefit to us of the cross. All our sickness and all our unhappiness can be brought to the cross so that we can be healed. He gladly bears our burden and we should not think that our sickness and unhappiness is some sort of trial from God. No, we should cast our burdens upon Jesus on the cross"

"XII. The twelfth station – Jesus dies on the cross. Before he dies He asks His Father to forgive those who are murdering Him – *Father forgive them for they know not what they do.* He appears to despair when He cries out, *My God, My God, why have you forsaken me?* But He is quoting Psalm 22 and He is doing so for our benefit. If you read this psalm it is almost an exact account of what is happening to Him on the cross. But the psalm ends in triumph and so it is not a moment of despair but a statement of the victory of the cross. Jesus is helping us in His final moments as He commends His spirit into the hands of God. Just before he dies Jesus cries *It is accomplished.* Then in one final act of submission He yields Himself completely to God – *Father into your hands I give my spirit.*"

At this point all of us kneel in front of the figure of the dead Jesus upon the cross. As we knelt for a while we let the full effects of the supreme sacrifice of Jesus permeate our being.

"XIII. The thirteenth station – Jesus is taken down from the cross. It was customary to break the legs of the crucified, in order to hasten their death but it was clear to the soldiers that Jesus was dead. It fulfils another prophecy that not one of his bones would be broken, So one of the soldiers pierced His side with a spear and out poured water. He had shed every drop of blood. Jesus gave everything for us, he bled to death. His body was taken down, probably with the same lack of respect shown earlier and then passed over to His mother and the apostle John for burial."

"XIV. The fourteenth station – Jesus is laid in the tomb. It seems that this is the end, as a huge stone is rolled in front of it to prevent his followers from stealing the body and claiming a false resurrection."

After completing our tour of the stations Giuseppe assembled us in a small clearing for one final address.

"My dear friends, I hope my Stations of the Cross have touched you. You will notice that there is no rising from the tomb shown in my stations. Of course I believe in the magnificent resurrection power of God and that this indeed did happen as verified by the many witnesses. But the Resurrection is NOT the victory by Jesus over sin and death. No! The cross is the total victory! It is on the cross that Jesus said, *it is accomplished* or *it is finished.* The full price is paid upon the cross, the victory has been achieved. The Resurrection is the fulfilment of that victory. I urge you again to meditate deeply upon the mysteries of the cross. For Jesus died NOT to make us better people but NEW people. He died on the cross NOT to change us but to EXCHANGE us! Exchange our sinful life for His resurrected life and that begins at the cross with the death of our old lives" The brother sighed as an indication that he too had given everything he had to give about his unique devotion.

"Brother Giuseppe, I thank you for the instruction you have given us this morning," said Joseph, "You have been truly blessed by the Holy Spirit and I thank you for sharing this devotion with us." And then he went on to ask the question which I wanted to ask but was too polite to do so. "Why have you chosen to live such a solitary life on this beautiful island, when you have so much insight into the Gospel, so much to give our needy world?"

"Ah my young friend you ask a difficult question and I must say that, despite what the sculler may have told you, I do welcome any visitor to this island who wishes to know more about the cross. I will happily share my thoughts with them, as I have done with you this morning. I was, for a long time, a serving monk in Rome. But I became disillusioned with the direction the Church there was taking. Too many sycophants and hangers on, who are gaining credence in that holy city and providing a ring of steel around the Pope. There is an unhealthy force abroad which is positively anti-Christian but I do not think the Holy Father is aware of how pervasive it has become!" He nodded sagely and then turning his head directed his final warning to me. "I caution you to have a care in your dealings with the flunkies that purport to act for the Pope. And take Father Peter's council at Abbazia di San Salvatore; he is a wise man and a true follower of Christ Jesus."

So, duly cautioned by the island's sage hermit, we said our goodbyes and embarked on the next part of our travels. Promptly, our sculler arrived and we tentatively stepped into the boat. Our precious cargo was handed from one to another and laid in the bow. I thought how we had never disclosed the full purpose of our trip to the monk nor shown him the volume. He had accepted us at face value and was satisfied with the bare explanation we had given him for our journey. I felt a little guilt that we had failed to confide in him as I felt he was completely trustworthy. We waved until the figure of Giuseppe disappeared from our sight and we were soon landed on the south side of the lake.

Two more days' journey ensued across the rolling Tuscan plains, roads hedged with Cyprus trees guided our way to the foothills of Monte Amiata and one final climb up to the monastery of San Salvatore.

Monte Amiata is a volcanic cone, which rises some two thousand feet above the surrounding plateau, making it quite a sizeable climb yet not as arduous as the Alpine mountains so recently conquered by us. But towards the end of a long walk across the plains, it still proved truly a test for us. Although quite some time since it last erupted, there are some thermal springs around its base which provided welcome reviving bathing for us all. For modesty's sake we let Gertrude bathe first and then, once dried and clothed, we three men took our turn. Beech and chestnut trees cover the lower slopes of Monte Amiata, and the higher slopes are covered with old growth forests that are spectacularly coloured in the autumn late sun and make the mountain extremely popular among hikers. We met several of them, out enjoying the scenery, who told us to beware of the many wolves which inhabit the area. Both the flora and fauna of these forests are unusually diverse, with a number of endemic species which I had never seen before. This made our trek up the hill enjoyable and before too long the outline of the monastery's campanile could be seen protruding above numerous buildings which comprised the adjoining town of San Salvatore. The town grew up following the establishment of the abbey and after negotiating its rather pleasant streets we arrived at the monastery door.

An aged monk responded to a summoning bell and led us into meet Abbot Peter, a tall bearded handsome man in his mid to late sixties. He invited us into his study and commanded our welcomer to bring some refreshment. Then in perfect English he addressed us,

"Welcome my friends from the cold, wet north east of England, we have been expecting you." We acknowledged his welcome whilst wondering how news of our coming could have preceded us. I felt Gertrude prickle a little at the Abbot's gibe about our inclement weather. Though on reflection he does have a point! "I have always had a love for your country and we have a mutual friend in Gregory. I met him a number of years ago in Rome and he has shared many stories about your land. News of your work, Bede, has travelled ahead of you and I knew that one day you would be before me as you are today." Then enigmatically he added, "*And we know that God works all things together for the good of those who love Him, who are called according to His purpose.* Now tell me your whole story before you show me the Codex "

We sat and painstakingly told him the account of what had happened, from my final meeting with Ceolfrith in his office in Monkwearmouth, to Kenric's heinous acts, to our encounter with Gregory and his instruction to take the Codex to Monte Amiata, then the flight over the Alps, our diversion to Isola San Guilio and our meeting with Giuseppe, right up to our arrival here at his monastery. Abbot Peter listened patiently, turning his attention to whichever speaker told their particular part of the story and then, when we had finished, addressed us,

"Ah Giuseppe is a holy man and his devotion of the Stations of the Cross is inspirational. It helped me look at the cross in a different way. I had always been taught to look at the cross and think – look what my sins have done to Jesus. But now I look at the cross and think – look what Jesus has done to my sin! This is a more powerful understanding of the cross and what Jesus accomplished on it. I have often asked Giuseppe to join our community, he would be a valuable asset to our monastery. We think the same way about the Church and the direction it is taking. But he is happy on that beautiful island – who wouldn't be? I have told him that he is always welcome here." Then he clasped his hands and stood up, imparting a sense of urgency. "Well! I've been patient for long enough. Your story is most interesting and more about that later but I can not wait any longer! Would you please show me the Codex?"

With that he swept out of his room assuming that we would follow in his wake; which we did. He led us to the library and made room on a table for the Codex to be placed. He carefully opened it and examined page after page in great detail. He took a magnifying glass from his pocket and scrutinised it even more thoroughly. I felt like a Jarrow schoolboy again, awaiting Godric's verdict on my homework. I hadn't long to wait for Abbot Peter's opinion.

"Bede! This is magnificent. Not only is it a work of art in itself but most importantly it is a God inspired translation of His Word." He sat as if poll axed and after gathering his thoughts he continued, "Gregory was absolutely correct in suggesting it be brought here. He will be a worthy custodian for the other copy on its journey to Rome. Though I am unsure if it will actually reach its destination. So much more important then, that this copy rests in our humble abbey and I would deem it an honour to guard it with my very life. This work will be a major influence on the spread of the Gospel throughout the world. We will use it to form the basis of translations in the vernacular so that all men and women, whatever language they speak, will be able to hear and in time, I hope, read it for themselves." He fixed his gaze on each of us before reaching the climax of his diatribe. "This is a dangerous concept for many in our Church and they will set their efforts against it and do whatever it takes to suppress your work. That is why I fear for the safety of the other volume and for Gregory, both of them on their way to Rome. Therefore it is vitally important that the whereabouts of this Codex is known only to you four and the occupants of this monastery. We are trustworthy men of like minds and forgotten by the hierarchy in Rome. They will never suspect that such a humble place could house such a treasure. In God's good time the volume will be revealed to the wider world."

We all agreed that this was the best possible course of action. Abbot Peter then told us about one of the inhabitants of the village who had a six seater carriage, which he used to transport people to and from the mountain. It had become quite an attraction and the villager made quite a good living from these tours and from the people who took them, which he had named - tourists.

"I have taken the liberty of arranging for him to take you to Rome, at our expense. So you will be able to complete the final part of your journey in relative comfort."

The delight on Gertrude's face at this news was tangible and we shared in the abbey's hospitality later that evening with a simple meal. Gertrude and I then took part in Compline, whilst Joseph and Odin retired early for the evening.

Chapter Fifteen
All Roads lead to Rome

Gertrude was in her element as the carriage drew alongside to pick us up with what little luggage we had. She gushed with enthusiasm as a stout, middle aged, balding man heaved heavy as he helped her up on to one of the seats. There were two long benches facing each other and probably able to accommodate up to three people on each of their leather bound cushioned seats with wooden back restraints. She motioned to the rest of us to follow her example and mount the wagon. After loading, Joseph and Odin hauled themselves up to sit opposite Gertrude with their backs to the driver. Meanwhile I stood next to the carriage in order to bid a final farewell to Abbot Peter, who had been joined by two of his confrères to witness our departure. The horse blew heavily in anticipation of its coming exertions and then pawed the the ground with its foot. The driver gently patted the animal in reassurance and then uttered comforting soothing sounds. Abbot Peter came towards me with his arms opened wide in welcome. He embraced me, then clasped my right hand with his own.

"Bede, my dear son. May the Lord himself go with you and may His love surround you. You must have a care in Rome and be circumspect in those you trust; no matter how elevated they may be within the Church. There are forces abroad that would see you harmed and the precious cargo, that Gregory is bearing, destroyed. Do not worry about the similar item which you have entrusted to my care. It will be guarded by our very lives and it will not leave this Abbey until God Himself deems it to be discovered. I remind you not to tell anybody, and I mean anybody, about your visit here. It must remain the most guarded of secrets, as the safety of the Codex is dependent upon it" He embraced me once more, as the other two monks smiled and nodded their approval. I knew by 'anybody', he meant His Holiness Pope Gregory the Second himself. I was to trust absolutely no one. I mounted the carriage unaided and took my seat next to my sister Gertrude, who I was still to pass off as my recently married wife. The driver gathered his reins and took his place in the vanguard of the carriage and, after waving to our former hosts, we moved off to begin our journey to Rome, the city eternal.

Communication with our aged pilot proved difficult as his Italian dialect was virtually impenetrable and he had no English at all. Added to the fact he was facing away from us, and the noise of the trundling cart, made conversation almost impossible. Thankfully Abbot Peter had instructed the driver well and he was already versed in making similar journeys and so this was no more than routine for him. We made banal conversation with each other regarding such English preoccupations as the weather and the local countryside, which was absolutely stunning. We descended the valley for almost two hours and the hazy outline of the seven hills of Rome soon loomed in the distance, perhaps fifteen or twenty miles away.

The traffic in carriages grew heavier, as did the foot passengers, along the road. Through sign language and gesticulations we were able to convince our friendly driver that we would like to break the journey for refreshment at the next available inn. As this approached, a group of four men could be seen making their way to the same comfort break. We recognised two of them as our friend Gregory and our adversary Kenric. The other two were the mysterious figures we had seen Kenric conversing with earlier, one was carrying luggage and the other a heavy satchel, very similar to the one which we had deposited with Abbot Peter at the Abbazia di San Salvatore, Monte Amiata. Presumably it was the other Codex! The driver pulled in to an area designated for the parking of vehicles next to the inn. After helping Gertrude descend the carriage, he indicated to us that he would attend to the horse whilst we took our refreshment. We left him to his chores and made our way to the inn, just in time to meet the party travelling by foot at the entrance to the building. It was Kenric who spoke first,

"Ah! It is our friends from the north. The glass merchants. Good day to you young lady and also to you my dear gentlemen. I trust that I find you all in good health and that all goes well with you?" Kenric's obsequious greeting was thick with false sincerity and was accompanied by ostentatious bowing. We returned his greeting with less enthusiasm, not wishing to alert Kenric to the fact that we were on more intimate terms with his travelling companion, Gregory, than he realised. Reluctantly we agreed to join them in some sustenance. We entered the inn which was packed full of carters and coopers seeking respite from their arduous day's work. Swarthy dark haired men, sweat glistening on their muscular arms, stood quaffing nut brown ale. With some difficulty we managed to find a table to accommodate our party plus Kenric and Gregory. The two menacing men found another one across from us and sat with their luggage and Codex next to them.

After ordering some drinks and a light snack Kenric then regaled us with the full details of their tortuous journey over the Alps and through the major northern Italian cities. Episodes were recounted and descriptions of the characters they had met were included. Kenric held forth, with the occasional word and grunt of confirmation from Gregory, who met our eyes with a sign of exhausted resignation. When, eventually, there was a lull in Kenric's conversation, when the maid came with our order, I felt that it required us to return details of our own journey. We were less forthcoming about the minutia. Instead I concentrated on the arduous journey we had undertaken through the Alps. Gertrude elaborated on the dangers we had encountered and I could see that Kenric was glad that they had taken the more meandering but less difficult route.

"My word young man, I am so glad that we did not come with you on your most challenging way. I am sure that your glass samples must have been at constant risk," said Kenric. He glanced from time to time across at his two accomplices, sat across the room at their own table. I could see that he was communicating to them subtly by means of a raised eyebrow or facial expression. All the time the satchel containing the Codex rested on a seat next to them. I realised that he would soon discover our lack of luggage and, not wishing him to become suspicious, decided that now would be an opportune time to offer an explanation. I noticed that Kenric's two companions sat silently glaring in our direction interrupted only by the occasional raising of glasses to their mouths.

"Yes Father Kenric we delivered our samples en route and hope to acquire much business for our glassworks in Monkwearmouth." I felt relieved that I had given him a plausible reason for our current state but I had underestimated his logic.

"So, what reason have you now to travel on to Rome? I mean if you have no more samples to show in that fine city then surely you can gain no further commercial advantage. Can you?" Worse than the substance of his question was the inquisitorial tone of his voice. I could sense that his innate cynicism led Kenric to question everyone and everything and, unless I could come up with a plausible reason for our lightness of luggage, he would begin to suspect our identities. It was too early yet to reveal our true status. I mumbled some incoherent erms and aghs and thankfully it was Gertrude who came to my rescue.

"My husband is too embarrassed, sir, to claim credit for his romantic suggestion." she smiled, gazing adoringly in my direction. "After concluding our business he surprised me by proposing that we visit Rome as, in truth, we have never had a honeymoon! He wishes to show me the sights of that historic city" I blushed crimson at this last statement which did have the advantage of total veracity. We certainly haven't had a honeymoon! I'd hoped that we would have been able to achieve our subterfuge without the necessity for lies and perhaps Gertrude's intervention was stretching this aspiration to its limits. She continued in the same false vein. "He even hired a carriage for the final part of our journey; see how much he cares for his own dear wife."

Noticing my obvious discomfort, and assuming this was the natural unease of a recently married groom, Kenric seemed satisfied at my sister's explanation. Her diversionary tactics were further enhanced as she made him a generous offer.

"We are sir within two hours travel of Rome and, as we have room on the carriage for two further passengers, I would like to invite you and your companion...Gregory is it?...to join us for this final part of the journey. We have sufficient room for your luggage and the large item in the satchel but I am afraid we do not have enough room for those other two men."

Brilliant! Brilliant, Gertrude, I thought. I could see Gregory's eyes light up in agreement as I stroked my chin, trying to appear nonchalant, and the suggestion met with approval from Kenric.

"You are very kind my lady, I would be most grateful to avail myself of your generous offer. I don't think that my poor feet can take much more of these Roman cobbles. I will arrange for Gregory and myself to stay at the Lateran Church community to the south of the city, if you would be kind enough to drop us off there."

I agreed to this course of action and I informed him that we would be staying at an hostelry near the Colosseum, not too far away from the Lateran Church. Dedicated to St. John, it was well known to me, having been my accommodation on some of my previous visits to Rome. But as I am disguised as a layman then a more common abode is required. Kenric, delighted with the arrangements then continued,

"Good, that's settled then. Please allow me a few moments to inform my two companions that they must continue their journey on foot and without our company. They have both been most helpful in transporting our belongings and I would like to give them a little money for all the trouble they have taken." Kenric excused himself and took the men outside for a private discussion, no doubt to include detailed conspiratorial instructions for some imminent dastardly action which he had in store for the Codex. This enabled us to converse with Gregory more informally than we had been able to so far. It was he who began,

"Well done Gertrude - good thinking. I've been looking over my shoulder for days now expecting them to strike. There was a moment in Milan when I thought they were going to do so but it was too busy with people for them to succeed. I think it is only because I have been taking my share in lugging the Codex and Kenric's bags that they haven't so far clobbered me. You wouldn't believe how heavy that thing is after a few hours! Also Kenric has been using the time to pump me for more information. You lot have come up more than once in our conversations. I think he suspects everyone; that's the sort of person he is but I think you have managed to throw him off the scent – for the time being at least! After we have settled in tonight at the Lateran we will make our way to the Vatican tomorrow with the Codex. I suggest that's the time we will confront him and have all this out. If all goes well we will have him and those two thugs arrested by the Vatican Guard and we will then present the Codex to the Holy Father."

We all assented to Gregory's plan as Kenric made his way back to our table, having concluded his business with the two conspirators. They did not return and I thought I detected a renewed air of suspicion from Kenric, as he saw our close huddle. Perhaps we over did the banter and small talk, in an attempt to convince him that we had been involved in only innocent mundane conversation whilst he was away. We attempted to settle the bill but Kenric insisted that he should pay. We then made our way to the carriage and the driver and horse stood obediently waiting our arrival. I explained, as best I could in my basic Italian, our two new additional passengers, as Odin and Joseph loaded their bags and the Codex satchel on to the rear of the vehicle. Although firmly secured by ropes, Joseph decided upon sitting on a makeshift seat above the luggage, in order to prevent the book from falling.

So, fully laden, our group began the ultimate part of our odyssey to Rome. We continued with our small talk and tried to engage with Kenric but he was uncharacteristically quiet and so our time passed unremarkably until we arrived at the Lateran church. The two clerical men disembarked from the carriage and were received into their temporary accommodation by an hirsute monk who tried to usher them in. Before doing so we arranged to meet the following morning near the entrance to the Colosseum at ten o'clock. I thought the welcoming monk showed me some recognition and, in an effort to maintain my cover, I curtly covered my face with my cloak and studiously ignored him. He, thinking he had been in error, continued with his ministrations to his new guests and deputed his assistant to help Gregory with the bags and the Codex. I saw Kenric in discussion with the monk as they walked towards the church. As if in possession of some new information, Kenric glanced over his shoulder in our direction.

We then made to our inn where, after registering our arrival, we said farewell to our driver after rewarding him generously for his safe transportation. That evening, during dinner, we met together to discuss our plan of action for the coming day. Gertrude impressed upon us that we were not to trust the arrangements we had previously made. She advised that we should expect the unexpected. As Odin's room was located in the attic area, with views overlooking the crumbling edifice of the Colosseum and up the hill to the Lateran Church, he was delegated to act as lookout for Gregory and Kenric.

Towards the end of our evening meal I decided to use the privy situated outside at the rear of the inn. Sanitation must be one of the greatest legacies of the Roman Empire and the toilets in Rome are amongst the best I have experienced. It was after relieving myself and, as I was washing my hands in a stone bowl with water from an earthen jug, that I was accosted by a tall bearded man who I instinctively recognised, despite the lack of light in the convenience. It was the more senior of the two men who had accompanied Kenric and Gregory. Grasping my tunic with his two hands he thrust me against the wall depriving me of breath. As I gasped in recovery, he released one of his hands from my garment. This relief was only to enable him to use this free hand to strike me a blow to the head. Anticipating the assault I was able to turn my face so that I did not receive the full frontal power of his punch. I was grateful for this small concession as the impact was severe enough for me to wince, as bright crimson liquid trickled from my nose. I wiped it with my arm and I was reminded of the Lord's exhortation to turn the other cheek. However, not wishing for any further punishment, I hung my head in shame as I listened in silence to his volley of abuse. In the interests of decorum I will précis his threat.

"A message from the Lord Kenric himself. Whoever the hell you are, he gives you a friendly warning. Mind your own business and keep out of things which don't concern you," he said. My head was swirling as the effects of the heavy blow started to take their toll. I stumbled and fell to the floor providing a suitable target for my assailants boot. He did not need any further invitation and I felt the weight of his kick into my midriff. "He has 'seen through' your glass merchant front." Buoyed up by his laughter at his own joke he shaped to give me another kick. He was only prevented from doing so by the sound of the familiar voice of Joseph.

"Hoy! Ger'off him. Now!" said my friend in his best Northumbrian accent, standing over my body to prevent further violation. Joseph was knocked off his feet and onto my torso as the assailant pushed past him and into the cover of outer darkness, throwing a scrap of something at me as he went. My friend helped me back to our table where Gertrude and Odin could only gape in horror as they saw me limp towards them. As I gingerly sat down I had recovered sufficient breath to explain what had just occurred.

"Our cover is blown. Kenric knows we are not who we said we were. I don't know if he knows who we are but I am afraid Gertrude, you were right. We must expect the unexpected. I suggest we keep a vigil watch during the night, as we did on our journey on the good ship Northumbria so many years ago. We will arise earlier than we had planned and prepare ourselves thoroughly for whatever Kenric has in store."

They all agreed and we arranged a programme of two hourly watches, Gertrude insisting that she take her turn. Odin's lofty perch was to be our look out post and he managed to borrow a spy glass telescope from the landlord. I unfurled the item my antagonist had thrown at me, which I had been clutching all the while. I recognised it as velum. Not just any velum but unmistakeably velum taken from animals grazing upon the lands at Monkwearmouth. Velum which I had used for the production of the Codex.

*   *   *   *   *   *

It must have been between three and four next morning when I was awoken by an excited Odin, shaking me violently in an effort to arouse me without disturbing the other guests.

"Bede! Bede wake up." he whispered, "Come, quickly and see." He tugged at my arm and I followed to his high room. "Here, look through this. Up the hill," he said, pointing through the window whilst handing me the telescope. "You can just make them out against the light of the moon."

I took the instrument from Odin and pointed it in the direction he was advising, up the hill towards the vicinity of the Lateran Church. There, coming down the lane, were the figures of three people. I turned the lens of the scope to adjust the focus and could discern the outline of Kenric, perhaps a mile or more away. Next to him I could perceive two men, one of whom I had encountered earlier that evening whilst the other struggled carrying a large satchel which I presumed to be the Codex. Gregory was notable by his absence.

"Right! Rouse the other two and tell them to get dressed and we'll meet downstairs." Less than five minutes later we had all assembled and I gave one final briefing before we left. "Be careful, they're dangerous. Don't take any risks, we'll let the authorities deal with them after we challenge them."

Like highly trained pugilists we all shook ourselves in readiness and crossed the lane outside our inn and made our way to the entrance to the Colosseum and awaited our opponents. It was a still, mild evening for the time of year, with the full moon illuminating the great arena and its environs. The silhouette of the three figures grew larger as they drew nearer our rendezvous point. It was Kenric who, trying to take advantage of the situation, spoke first.

"Ah my young friends, how strange to find you all here at this time of day or is it still night? My colleague told me of his encounter with you earlier and I am surprised to see you once again, to say the least." He smirked in recognition of my black eye which had erupted since my earlier assault. I stepped forward from the crowd of my friends in an attitude of bravado and, drawing myself to my full height, spoke slowly and deliberately.

"Sir! As I am sure that you are now aware, I am not, nor have ever been, a glass merchant. This dear lady is not my wife but my sister. I am sir, Bede! I am a monk in the order, as you are, of St Benedict. My sister Gertrude is a nun in the self same order. My mother house is the Monastery of St Peter Monkwearmouth and I am the author of the Codex, the very item your colleague is now carrying in his satchel. My former abbot the late Ceolfrith commissioned me to write it, at the behest of His Holiness Pope Gregory and it is our purpose to submit this work to the former Pope's successor and namesake."

I could see from Kenric's reaction that, although not cognisant of all the details, my admission confirmed the unspoken suspicions he had harboured for a long time. Before he could muster a reply I purposed to continue and drive home my objective.

"I believe my Lord Kenric that you, through your dastardly intermediaries here, are responsible for my dear friend Ceolfrith's death, as well as the untimely passing of the two hands lost aboard the Angel of Northumbria."

"I suppose you will no doubt wish to add the life of your colleague Gregory to my indictments." he interrupted, "He now lies dangerously sick under the ministrations of the brothers at the Lateran. But I am afraid accusations and proof of those accusations are two different things." A smirk of smug self satisfaction crossed his face as he parried my recriminations.

"Well, we'll see what the authorities have to say about it." I countered. Then in an attempt to bluff my way through I continued, "We have alerted the Vatican Guard and we intend to hand you over to them. We will let them examine the evidence we have accumulated and I am sure that they will come to the same conclusion we have."

Kenric stood impassively, mentally computing the information I had disclosed. He was not about to succumb easily to my arguments. Meanwhile his two henchmen became noticeably more nervous, moving uneasily from side to side and glancing around to see if they were about to be apprehended. I motioned to Odin and Joseph to move forward in support.

"First of all Kenric, instruct your man there to hand the Codex over to Joseph. It is an affront to all that's holy that you should be in receipt of my work."

That was the trigger for the accomplice with the book to dart into the dark entrance of the Colosseum and disappear from sight. The senior stronger rogue burst forward towards me and it took both Odin and Joseph to restrain him from finishing the job he started the previous evening. Meanwhile Gertrude took it upon herself to pursue the absconder. It wasn't long before we realised that this was to be up the terraced interior to the top of the arena. This was confirmed when the figure of the villain appeared precariously on the rim of the Colosseum. He aimed a volley of incoherent abuse at us from his airy vantage point with a background of black sky, punctuated by stars. His friend struggled vainly to release himself from Odin and Joseph's grip as Kenric looked on anxiously.

That anxiety was shared by we three northern contingent when Gertrude suddenly appeared to confront the Codex toting criminal. She tugged at the straps of the satchel but her adversary was too strong for her and, rather ungentlemanly, kicked out at her sending her over the side of the Roman amphitheatre. My heart leapt as I saw her clutch on to the rim and she was left dangling helplessly over the edge. Instinctively Odin released his grip on the reprobate down below and ran up to her aid. The accomplice above showed no mercy for his stranded pursuer and laughed in derision as he tried to make good his escape. However Gertrude had weakened the straps of the satchel which began to break away from the main body of the bag. This unbalanced its carrier and he tottered perilously and, in an attempt to save his own life, he jettisoned the Codex over the side. Instead of stabilising himself, this action seemed to have the opposite effect and, after moving from leg to leg and stretching out his arms to steady his swaying body, he lost the battle! As if in slow motion his body tumbled, head over heels, above us onlookers. He must have made two, three hundred and sixty degree, turns before his body crashed with a sickening thud on to the ground twenty metres away. A pool of blood oozed from his head, staining the grass a rich claret colour. Selfishly I turned my attention to my sister whose predicament had been improved by the arrival of Odin who was now hauling her back to safety.

In concert with the plunging body of the ill fated man, was the course of the book. Kenric preferred to follow the progress of the descending Codex rather than his tumbling henchman. Breaking away from our party he'd ran towards the anticipated landing area, repeating as he went, 'the book...the book.' My attention had been drawn first to the progress of the human object and I had closed my eyes as his body's fall was broken by the hard ground. I had opened them just in time to see the Codex strike Kenric a glancing but fatal blow to his left temple.

In the throws of death he had somehow managed to snatch a page from the Codex and he held it towards me. Assessing that one man lay dead and another dying, I decided my time would be more use to the latter. Kenric was still conscious as I knelt next to him. My attempts to administer the last rites to the injured cleric were disturbed as I was unceremoniously pushed to one side by my former aggressor who had broken free from Joseph's grasp. He scooped up the Codex in his arms like a baby and sprinted into the night. I prevented Joseph from following, telling him he would be more use helping Odin rescue Gertrude. He complied with my suggestion and left me to attend to Kenric, who was now mouthing something. I realised he was asking me to read the extract from the page he had torn, in his frenzy, from the Codex. I duly obliged. The particularly apt extract was from the Gospel of St. Mark and my words broke through the silence of the early morning like a herald of the dawn.

"Jesus said to them, "Have you never read in the Scriptures: 'The stone the builders rejected has become the cornerstone. This is from the Lord, and it is marvellous in our eyes' Therefore I tell you that the kingdom of God will be taken away from you and given to a people who will produce its fruit. He who falls on this stone will be broken to pieces, but he on whom it falls will be crushed." I placed the page on his chest and looked into his eyes.

"Kenric! Repent of your sins now and throw yourself upon the Lord's mercy." I swear I saw a glimmer of recognition in his eyes, a flicker of repentance, a sign he was sorry for his sins. I saw the light of life leave those eyes too and I gently closed his eyelids and, taking a phial of holy oils from within my tunic, I traced the sign of the cross on his forehead and prayed for his immortal soul.

My three companions soon joined me and we engaged in a four way hug of relief that we were all still in one piece.

"The Codex Bede!" panted Odin "Could you not have stopped him Joseph?" Before he could reply I interrupted.

"It's OK Odin I told him to help you two. You are both more important than the Codex. I'll warrant that's the last we'll see of it. Perhaps it was destined never to reach the Pope at all."

I stood momentarily musing upon what I'd just said, then gathered more of my thoughts and continued.

"Most importantly now, is the health of our dear friend Gregory. If what Kenric said about his illness is true I would suggest that he has been about his deadly poisoning again. There is no time to be lost." Clapping my hands as if to draw a line under what had taken place I started to direct operations. "Can you three attend to this mess? Report what has taken place to the authorities and have the bodies removed. Tell them about the theft too and give them a description of Kenric's accomplice. I am afraid this will take some time so I will away to the Lateran to see Gregory."

Then, as if to reassure them about the fate of our old friend, I quoted the words of the great evangelist John's Gospel I had used before, "This sickness will not end in death. No, it is for God's glory so that God's Son may be glorified through it."

So, I left my sister and two friends to fulfil my instructions and ran up the hill to the Lateran Church. Although now nearly five in the morning I knew that there would be someone up preparing for the first service of the day. My explanation was received with recognition from the monk I had been so rude to the previous day and I was duly shown into Gregory's simple cell where he lay, clearly dying. His face was pale and wan and he displayed all the symptoms of poisoning. I knelt by the side of his bed, tears streaming down my cheeks. I must have been kneeling there for almost two hours before the cell door opened and my sister and friends joined me. They had completed their statements to the authorities and the bodies had been removed to a mortuary pending burial. Gertrude seeing my state of distress embraced me and, thanks be to God, was responsible for quickening my faith.

"Bede," she said gently, "remember what you said about this sickness not ending in death. Those were the words of the Lord Jesus Himself, I believe, when informed of His own dear friend Lazarus' sickness." She raised me from my knees and sat me down in the corner, she had not finished her evangelising yet. " Remember too the words of of the apostle James, ' Is anyone among you sick? Let them call the elders of the church to pray over them and anoint them with oil in the name of the Lord.' We are those elders, the four of us! And Jesus said, 'Again, truly I tell you that if two of you on earth agree about anything they ask for, it will be done for them by my Father in heaven.' So come on Bede! Let us act out our faith!"

These were just the words I needed to hear. So we all laid hands on

Gregory and commanded the poison to come out of him in Jesus' name. We took it in turns to watch and pray. The morning passed into the afternoon and the afternoon into night. Then a full twelve hours after we first prayed, and almost twenty four hours since he must have received the poison, Gregory was violently sick. His fever seemed to subside and he slept more peacefully. By now we had all reassembled in his cell and sleep came to us too. We were awakened by a familiar voice asking why on earth we were sleeping on the floor of his room?

Our joy was complete as our Lazarus was restored to us and we then related the full details of our past thirty six hours' exploits to our risen friend. Gregory was saddened at the death of our adversaries, showing great compassion. He said he always felt diminished by the death of someone he had been unable to impart the gift of salvation to. He was also sorry that we had to face such calamities without his help. A messenger from Pope Gregory himself arrived to suggest that Gregory should complete his recuperation at the Pope's own summer residence at Castel Gandolfo on the shores of Lago di Albano to the south of Rome. We too were invited to join our friend for the duration of his stay.

So for the following three days we enjoyed an idyllic time staying at the Pope's summer residence where we spent our mornings walking next to the lake. Although the early Italian winter was mild, it was still too cold for bathing, though Joseph and Odin did 'plodge' (as we northerns call it) in the icy water. They ran out of the water quicker than they ran in. Gertrude and I meanwhile were firmly shore based. The lake was beautiful, shimmering in the low winter sun. Joseph sarcastically suggested that if I ever were to get married then this would be an ideal venue for it. I told them that my married days were well and truly behind me!

One day we were honoured to meet the Pope himself who asked us to give a full account of our expedition to Rome. This I did from my meeting with Ceolfrith up to and including the resurrection from near death of our friend Gregory. The only omissions were the locations of the Codex Amiatinus and the Codex Jarrow. Pope Gregory listened attentively and in silence, taking in every detail of my recount, and before replying he sent his attendants out of the room to ensure that he was alone with us.

"My dear English friends, you have indeed worked tirelessly for the sake of the Gospel and in pursuit of justice for your dead friends. But you must have realised by now, that there are forces in our Church that are not in support of the establishment of God's Kingdom here on earth. In fact they are in league with the Antichrist and are committed to the overthrow of all that is holy. The evangelist John told us this would happen in his book of Revelation or the Apocalypse. We are not fighting against flesh and blood but the heinous forces of Satan, using gullible people for their own evil ends. We are aware of their activities within the Vatican itself and we are determined to root them out. The production of your most holy book is an affront to their sensibilities and they were always going to undermine its transportation to our presence. Unfortunately our investigations have drawn a blank as to the whereabouts of the volume or its thief. Although you have not alluded to the fact, we are aware that two further copies were also commissioned. We do not hold any recriminations for you not admitting this in your account to us. You do right in keeping the whereabouts of the holy books a secret, which must accompany all who know it to their graves! We hope that this is a long time in the future. However in God's good time, when it is most opportunistic, their locations will be revealed to a needy world."

The Pope invited us to stay as long as we wanted and then bade us farewell with all good wishes and arrangements were made for our departure from Italy. Passage was booked on a boat which would deposit us at Dover. From there we would make our way to Canterbury to report our findings to the archbishop before returning to Monkwearmouth.

Kenric and his associate were given the honour of a Christian burial in Rome, with the Church not passing judgement on them but preferring to give them the benefit of the mercy of God. The service took place quietly in a private chapel in the catacombs, a riddle of underground passage ways traversing the city of Rome. Used by the early Christians as a burial ground and hideaway in times of persecution, it now houses two English corpses, their lives only a passing memory. Before setting sail for home we were the only witnesses to their interment.

Chapter Sixteen
At The Well

It is now six months since we arrived home. We have celebrated the Lord's birth at Christmas and His death and resurrection at Easter. We are now in my favourite season of Pentecost when we remember how the Holy Spirit fell on the apostles and empowered them to preach the Gospel.

When we arrived in Dover we then reported our exploits to the Archbishop of Canterbury before returning to Monkwearmouth. He was horrified to hear about the events leading up to Kenric's death. The archbishop had long suspected Kenric of undermining his authority but lacked the proof to hold him to account. However he had no idea of the utter depravity his former aide had sunken to. He could not comprehend how a so called man of God could resort to murder. Although Kenric had not actually sullied his hands with the blood of his victims, the archbishop held him no less responsible for Ceolfrith, Henry and Stephen's deaths and the attempted murder of Gregory. He drew the parallel with David in the Old Testament who was responsible for Uriah the Hittite's death. Desiring Uriah's wife Bathsheba (whom David had made pregnant) he tried to cover up his mistake by pretending the child was her husband's. But as, out of loyalty to David, Uriah had not slept with his wife he knew his infidelity would soon be discovered. So, David sent Uriah back to the front line of war. He instructed his generals to withdraw when attacked by the enemy, leaving Uriah without support and facing certain death. Although David had not actually physically harmed Uriah, God still held him responsible for murdering him.

The archbishop said he would make known Canon Kenric's perfidious behaviour and would expunge his name from the noble records of the Church in England. He also took to heart the Pope's words about the insidious force which was pervading our Church and he determined to redouble his efforts to put his house in order. He felt the best way of doing so was to rededicate the church in England to the Gospel of Jesus Christ.

We returned home buoyed up by the archbishop's exhortations which we passed on to our own Abbot Hwaetberht. All this time we studiously kept our own council about the whereabouts of the Codex which we had entrusted to the monks of Abbazia di San Salvatore, Monte Amiata. And, of course, I am the only person who knows where the third copy of the Codex is.

But now you find me in this Pentecost season at the ruins of the Roman fort Arbeia in South Shields. It is that time of the year when we hold our annual kickbladder competition. Odin's son Mika and his teammate Penelope are holding the cup aloft having just beaten Felling 4 -3 in an exciting final. This is the first time since the inaugural competition, which was won by our old team, that the Heb Burn team has won the cup. The competition has grown over the years and many more teams have entered, making it a more difficult tournament to win. Our team has succeeded in getting to the final on a number of occasions but has never won since that first victory. We have long since hung our boots up but have always taken an interest in how our successors were doing.

Abbot Hwaetberht, in recognition of the recent traumatic events, asked me to take a sabbatical year to reflect spiritually and to have more of a rest physically before resuming my scholarly work. So, as I have had more time at my disposal, I suggested to Odin and Joseph that we take over the running of the team and prepare them for the competition. I am glad to say that we have lost none of the old kickbladder magic. It has been a great relief spending time training the girls and boys and it was pleasing to see an equal balance of the sexes in our squad. Mika and Penelope are joint captains of what is a much more talented team than ours was.

"We've done it again Bede!" shouted Odin. "I think you and Joseph deserve all the credit. You've both given more time to the training than I've been able to. Well done!"

"No, no Odin, your contribution was brilliant," said Joseph, "all credit to Bede though for getting the old team together again. We're too old to play but we've still got the knowledge."

"We've all done good lads! It's been a great way to blow those cobwebs away," I said, giving my two fellow managers a high five. "Kickbladder is a great leveller, it truly is the beautiful game. It's just a pity we couldn't have Henry and Stephen playing and Ceolfrith to present the trophy."

After a few quiet moments of reflection we rejoined the rest of the team and their families to continue with the celebrations. Mother was present to cheer on Joseph's and Odin's children and her surrogate grandchildren. Gertrude attended to her and took her to the tent which had been erected to provide after match refreshments. As they made their way in an orderly queue, I slipped away from the throng.

Making the three mile journey back to St. Paul's Monastery Jarrow I decided to take a detour to my well. This well of holy waters, which has been a source of spiritual sustenance to me over the years, has been particularly important to me these past months. My time of reflection has been a time also of revelation. I have spent periods here alone with my thoughts, reflecting on the events of the past year which have had such a profound effect upon me. Although I am a man in excess of forty summers in age, I feel I lost some of my innocence on my last visit to Rome investigating Ceolfrith's death and attempting to convey the Codex, my great Opus Dei, to the Pope. Although I had been familiar with the concept of a devil and Satan as an evil force, I think this was my first encounter with an actual manifestation of such a dark influence in human form. Perhaps I had been naïve or too innocent in the past and had rationalised away this malevolent dominion. I did not have any real experience of this negative power. But I am under no illusion now. We are involved in a very real battle between good and evil and this conflict is being played out in even the most mundane of arenas. Often our wolf like adversaries disguise themselves in sheep's clothing and we must be vigilant at all times.

But I do not wish to dwell too much on an adversary that is both inadequate and defeated. It is sufficient to be aware of our enemy and that he will flee from us if we resist him. As Jesus says though, we must not rejoice that the devils submit to us but rather rejoice because our names are written in Heaven. This is how I have been building myself up in this sabbatical year, this time of holy writ. I have been concentrating on submitting my life totally to the will of God and this holy well is one of the places where I feel God's presence with me. From the earliest encounter with that angelic being, which my father knew to be the initial call on my life, until today I have been in reverence and awe whenever I have spent a season seeking God here. He has never let me down, revealing His will for me. I know that today if I listen to His voice He wishes to draw me to Him. As I kneel by those cooling waters I cup my hands and drink. I immerse my head as if in baptism and feel that healing balm. I am prompted in my spirit to recall those words from the Letter to the Hebrews:

Therefore, brethren, since we have confidence to enter the holy place by the blood of Jesus, by a new and living way which He inaugurated for us through the veil, that is, His flesh, and since we have a great priest over the house of God, let us draw near with a sincere heart in full assurance of faith, having our hearts sprinkled clean from an evil conscience and our bodies washed with pure water. Let us hold fast the confession of our hope without wavering, for He who promised is faithful; and let us consider how to stimulate one another to love and good deeds, not forsaking our own assembling together, as is the habit of some, but encouraging one another; and all the more as you see the day drawing near.

An hour or even two must have passed between me and the Lord beyond the veil. I feel ransomed, healed, restored, forgiven. I raise myself from a prone position and make my way to Jarrow. From the hill I can see my friends and family awaiting my arrival. The children chasing Gertrude and one another, squealing with excitement. Joseph and Odin beckon me towards them as mother smiles, whilst holding a neighbour's child in her arms. I run down the grassy bank and cradle my family and my friends in a loving embrace. Once again I am home.

I recall, dear reader, that I have not as yet disclosed the secret location of my Codex. The one Ceolfrith commanded that I should hide and disclose its location to absolutely no one! Well my friend, can I trust you? Can you keep a secret unto the grave?

You can....well then.......so can I!

Postscript

Pope Gregory did commission the Codex
and Ceolfrith charged that three copies be made

Ceolfrith did die in France en-route to Rome

He was succeeded by Hwaetberht as Abbot of Monkwearmouth

There is no evidence of the Codex ever reaching Rome

The Codex later appears in the 9th century at the Abbey of the Saviour,
Monte Amiata in Tuscany (hence the description 'Amiatinus'), where it
remained until 1786 when it passed to the Laurentian Library in Florence
This is the only evidence of the Codex today

Wilfred was Bishop of Northumbria

Some historians believe there is evidence that Bede was married!
Although most scholars refute this claim

There are Stations of the Cross on the island of
San Guilio in the middle of Lago di Orta Italy

Bede went on to be a great scholar, historian and theologian

Bede's Way is a footpath between St. Paul's Church Jarrow and
St. Peter's Church Monkwearmouth Sunderland. It is a glorious route
tracing the saint's footsteps between the two monasteries.

The Jarrow Codex has never been discovered

Other Books By The Author

The Bede Trilogy

Bede's Well – The Boyhood of Bede

Bede's World – The Youth of Bede

Bede's Way – The Manhood of Bede

Faith Books

What The Church Won't Tell You About: The Cross

What The Church Won't Tell You About: Healing

What The Church Won't Tell You About: Faith

What The Church Won't Tell You About: Mercy

What The Church Won't Tell You About: Grace

What The Church Won't Tell You About: Prayer

What The Church Won't Tell You About: The Devil

What The Church Won't Tell You About: God

Novels

Insurable Interest – A Thriller

Poor Banished Children of Eve – Set in Victorian England

A Man After My Own Heart – David of Israel

15 Minute Short Stories – Thirteen Short Stories

More Information

www.joeestewart.weebly.com

26246345R00085

Printed in Poland
by Amazon Fulfillment
Poland Sp. z o.o., Wrocław